Everyone knows the story of Jack and the beanstalk. Everyone also knows that Jack's little adventure made him a very rich man. But what they don't know is what happened a long time after Jack. . . .

Don't miss the upcoming Further Tale:

The Brave Apprentice

The Thief and the Beanstalk

P. W. CATANESE

ALADDIN PAPERBACKS
NEW YORK   LONDON   TORONTO   SYDNEY

This book is a work of fiction. Any references to historical
events, real people, or real locales are used fictitiously. Other
names, characters, places, and incidents are the product of
the author's imagination, and any resemblance to actual events
or locales or persons, living or dead, is entirely coincidental.

ALADDIN PAPERBACKS
An imprint of Simon & Schuster Children's Publishing Division
1230 Avenue of the Americas, New York, NY 10020
Copyright © 2005 by P. W. Catanese
All rights reserved, including the right of reproduction
in whole or in part in any form.
ALADDIN PAPERBACKS and colophon are registered
trademarks of Simon & Schuster, Inc.
Designed by Tom Daly
The text of this book was set in Adobe Jenson.
Manufactured in the United States of America
First Aladdin Paperbacks edition May 2005
2 4 6 8 10 9 7 5 3 1
Library of Congress Control Number 2004107563
ISBN 1-4169-0600-2

For Kristina, Michael, and Andrew

Nick opened his eyes and blinked. He felt the warmth of decaying straw rising from below and cool autumn air penetrating from above. But it was an unpleasant sensation that woke him: three points of cold metal pressing into his throat, chest, and belly. He thought of the pitchfork, always propped against the wall near the barn door.

"Get up," a familiar voice said.

"How c-can I?" Nick replied. He knew there was fear in his voice, but that was all right. The man holding the pitchfork might take pity.

"Show your face, then," the voice growled. He prodded with the pitchfork as he spoke.

Nick whimpered. He was sure the middle tine had pierced the skin on his chest. He could feel his heart hammering under the wound. Moving cautiously, he reached up and pushed the straw away, revealing his dirt-smudged face.

The farmer glared down at Nick's thin nose, brown

eyes, and tangled mop of dark hair. Nick had watched this man from hiding for nearly a month now. But the farmer had never known Nick was there until now.

"Oh, Geoffrey, it's just a boy!" said a second voice. The farmer's wife stood behind her husband, holding an enormous knife.

"Just a boy? Just a thief, you mean. Stealin' the food from our mouths." He wiggled the pitchfork as he spoke, and the pain in Nick's chest flared at all three points. Nick squeezed his eyes shut and pulled his lips back from clenched teeth.

"How long you been around here?" the farmer said.

"A couple of days," Nick lied.

"Days?" The farmer laughed bitterly. "A month is more like it. That's when the chickens stopped layin' so many eggs. And the cow stopped givin' so much milk. And the turnips and onions started to disappear. Ain't it?"

"Please—you're hurting me!" Nick said. He had seen the farmer's cruel nature as he watched from hiding these past weeks: beating the dog, cursing at his wife, twisting the neck of a rooster that pecked his ankle too many times.

"I'll do worse than hurt," the farmer said. There was an angry spark in his eye.

"Now, Geoffrey," said the wife. "We can't just kill him, can we?" From the tone of her voice, Nick thought this was a question of practicality, not morals. Would they get in trouble? Would they get caught?

"This little rat won't be missed. I'll cut him up and fatten our pigs on the pieces. Get back what's ours, we will!" The pitchfork drew back and came down again for the killing thrust. But Nick reached up from the straw and grabbed the pitchfork between the tines. He shoved it to one side, and the points plunged deep into the pile, inches from his gut. The farmer pulled back on the fork with a grunt and Nick held on, scrambling to his feet, with yellow strands of straw flying into the air. Chickens and geese squawked and flapped around the barn, and the cow turned to watch with mild interest.

With a savage scream, the farmer twisted the pitchfork, wrenching it from Nick's hands. Nick darted the other way, only to see the wild-eyed wife coming at him with the enormous knife. Nick had to duck to avoid the slash. He dropped to all fours and scampered underneath the cow. Looking back, he could see two pairs of legs coming around opposite sides of the animal. He shot back under the belly again and raced through the open door into the pale light of dawn.

"I'll get you yet!" the farmer shouted. But Nick knew the race was over. The farmer had a bad leg that would not straighten, and could only hobble along in slow pursuit.

Nick felt his sweat stinging in the three wounds, and a white-hot anger flooded through him. He picked up a stone and flung it at the farmer. "You can't kill me if you can't catch me, old man!"

The farmer threw his arms in front of his face and the

stone flew over his shoulder. He pointed at Nick. "You better run, little thief! Run while you can. We'll set the dogs on you, my neighbors and me! We're comin' after you! Thief! Wretch!" He went on shouting until Nick was too far to hear him anymore.

Nick dashed across fields and hopped a stone wall. When he was out of sight at last from the bellowing farmer, he changed directions to avoid pursuit, heading away from the rising sun.

An hour later, he came to a stream. He sat on a large rock and pulled his ragged tunic up, tucking it under his chin. The wound on his chest was still bleeding. He cupped water in his hand and splashed it onto the gash.

Nick looked down at the ribs that were plain to see under his skin, and the shrunken space where other boys had plump bellies. He was not quite the skeleton that had crawled onto the farm a month ago and began to drink the eggs raw, and lay under the cow to squeeze its milk into his open mouth. But he was still terribly thin.

He had lost more than a hiding place; he'd had to leave behind the sack of items he'd stolen over time. They were things of meager value—a ceramic bottle, a pewter spoon, bits of colored glass, buttons, a buckle without a belt, a brass thimble, a toy horse made of wood—but he might have traded them for something to eat.

Nick wondered how long he could last before he found another source of food. Shivering a little in the cool morning, he wondered also where he would take shelter from colder days to come. He let the tunic fall back to his knees and turned toward the sun. *Might as well go west,* he thought. *The sea is out there somewhere. I'd like to see that. Maybe get on a ship, go far away from here.*

The sea was nowhere in sight now, though. From this spot, it looked like heading west would bring him to a high, wild land. There were no roads or trails, no visible farms or towns, no smoke rising from chimneys. At the far horizon stood a rocky ridge. Maybe on the other side there was a better place.

A dim sound floated toward Nick from the direction he had fled: A dog barking—and more dogs echoing the cry.

He leaped across the stream and ran toward the wilderness.

● CHAPTER 2 ●

He did not care if the legend was true or not. The only thing that mattered was the fortune.

"If we can find a way to get inside, there's enough gold in there to make us rich as princes," said Finch.

The two men observed the great house as it gleamed under the full moon. They were hidden in the inky undergrowth at the forest edge. Finch was by far the bigger of the pair, handsome and powerfully built, with a neatly trimmed mustache and a little triangle of a beard. His companion was a dirty gnome of a man called Squint.

There were twelve altogether in Finch's band of thieves. Finch was careful about whom he enlisted. He preferred his men strong, fast, and deadly with weapons. Slightly built Squint was the exception, but there was a reason. Feeble as his body was, his acute eyesight had proven valuable to the band on many occasions. Finch was counting on Squint now to help him see a way into Old Man Jack's house.

House? Fortress is a better word for this place, thought Finch. It was not nearly as big as some of the impressive castles he had seen here and there in his wanderings, or the one he had been driven from years before. But in this remote area, it was the largest structure for many miles around.

Yet the purpose of its architecture was not to be big; the intent was to be impenetrable. There was only one entrance, a massive wood and iron door that looked sturdy enough to defy a battering ram. There were windows high and low, but they offered little promise. The low ones were narrow slits, crossed by heavy bars. The upper windows were wider but far out of reach, nearly forty feet off the ground.

The house was built on a gently rising hill. The slope and the flat fields around it were kept clear of bushes and trees, making it difficult to approach unseen. At all times, a sentry patrolled the top of the walls, slowly pacing the square perimeter.

All of this worried Finch, but encouraged him at the same time. *That means there's something inside worth protecting,* he thought.

"So you really believe that story, about the giant and the beanstalk?" asked Squint, glancing sideways at his leader. Squint was nervous, and Finch knew why. Breaking into strongholds was not the band's usual way; waylaying hapless travelers was more to its liking.

"Of course I don't believe it," snapped Finch. "But what does it matter anyway? I don't care where his wealth came from. I just want it to be mine."

Squint turned his peering eyes back to Jack's house, but went on talking. "It could be true, though, couldn't it? Think about it. Jack was just a lad when it happened—*if* it happened. Now he might be the oldest man in these parts. So everyone who might have seen it happen is dead, and only the story is left. And you know how stories are: They get told, stranger to stranger, father to son, and they change a bit every time they're passed along. Before long you don't know what's real and what's rubbish."

Finch had no patience for this speculation. The wealth inside those white stone walls was a siren calling to him. "Listen, Squint. This Jack is just a crazy old bird with nothing better to do than make up stories about himself that only fools like you believe. Now I've got a story for you: He's rich. We're not. The end. So shut up and find me a way inside."

"I think I already have," said Squint. "But we have to get closer."

Finch nodded. He reached to the ground and picked up a lantern that was covered with metal doors to conceal its glow. Finch kept it close to his belly and turned his back to Jack's house, to shield the light from the sentry. Then he opened and closed one of the hinged doors three times.

At the wood's edge a few hundred yards to the north, two more of Finch's men saw the signal. They began to make noise, shaking branches and mimicking the sounds of forest animals. The disturbance had the desired effect, as the sentry went over to that side of the castle wall.

"Let's go," said Finch. With Finch leading the way, the two cutthroats broke from the cover of the trees and headed for the fortress. The moonlight illuminated them as they ran, but the distracted sentry did not see them and they safely reached the darkness at the foot of the white stone walls. Squint's breathing was labored from the sprint. But Finch had the predatory strength of a wolf, and the exertion did not affect him at all.

"Now tell me—when the time comes, how do we get in?" said Finch.

"I thought . . . these might . . . be the answer. Now I'm not . . . so certain," wheezed Squint, struggling to catch his breath. With a gnarly finger, he pointed at the ivy that snaked up to the highest reaches of the wall.

"These vines? No man could ever climb them, you dolt! Look how flimsy they are!" Finch was outraged that they had made the risky dash to this spot for no good reason. He gave a hard yank on one of the vines, and it peeled from the wall with a sound like ripping fabric.

"Yes, yes. I can see that, now that we're close," said Squint. "They couldn't support a grown man. But what if we got a kid to climb up there and unlock the big door for us? That's the answer, isn't it?" Squint narrowed his eyes and looked at Finch, waiting with an expectant grin.

Finch worked his jaw side to side and tugged the

short hairs of his beard, thinking it over. He gave one of the sturdier vines a gentler tug. It clung fast to the walls, where its tiny threadlike fingers penetrated the cracks and seams of the stone.

"Yes. That is the answer," he said. "All we need is a little thief to do some climbing." He smiled. With his hands to the stone, he could practically feel Jack's treasure through the walls.

A few minutes later Finch's men created another distraction. They stumbled out of the woods, arms across each other's shoulders, singing loudly and badly like a drunken pair of peasants. High atop the walls, the sentry watched them, amused. Finch and Squint ran unseen back to the shadows of the forest, heading for the hidden lair of the band of thieves.

Finch dreamed about Jack's gold all night. His greedy desires woke him early the next morning, before the forest was fully sunlit. He dressed in fine clothes, stolen from some noble victim waylaid long before. Then he packed food and blankets into a leather bag. He was prepared to spend several days if necessary to find the boy he needed.

Finch roused the rest of the band from their crude tents, kicking the ones who woke too slowly. The men were drowsy and angry, but they feared Finch too much to complain. It was cool on that late summer morning. The eleven thieves gathered close around the campfire to hear what Finch would say. Squint stirred the hissing coals and threw on new wood. Sparks flew up and died amid the rising smoke.

"We've discovered the way into Jack's fortress," said Finch, his face red in the fire's glow. "So I'm off to recruit a new member of our gang. A temporary member, you might say." Finch drew his favorite object in the world from the sheath at his hip: a large jagged knife, kept dangerously sharp. He ran his finger along the face of the blade as he spoke.

"Now listen carefully. There is to be no thieving, no robbing, no murdering, no nothing, until I get back here with a boy. We're new to these woods, so nobody's worried about us yet, and that's just the way I want it. Does everyone understand that?"

There were groans of displeasure. One of the band spoke up—a hairy, bearish man with a tangled black beard, named Pewt.

"What's this all about, Finch? Ever since we got here, you've gone on about this Jack and his treasure. There's easy pickings in these woods. We've seen travelers with all kinds of goodies on the forest road, just waiting for us to nab them. What are we waiting for? Why don't we . . ."

Pewt let his words trail off when he saw the stare Finch had fixed on him. Finch tilted his head forward and brought his eyebrows down to cast a shadow around his icy blue eyes. Pewt tried to return the look, but soon decided he would rather examine the dirt at his feet. The two gang members closest to him took a step away, not wanting to gain a share of Finch's wrath.

For a long uncomfortable moment, Finch kept his gaze fixed on Pewt. Then at last he looked up and spoke again.

"I said, does everyone understand that?"

This time there were grunts and murmurs of agreement.

"Toothless John, you're in charge while I'm gone. See that my orders are obeyed. And deal with disobedience however you like." Finch shot a final scowl at the red-faced Pewt, who regarded the ground below with renewed interest.

Toothless John stood at Finch's side with his arms crossed. Of all of Finch's brutish collection of thugs and cutthroats, he was the most vile. He stood a head taller than the rest and never met a man who could look him straight in the eye. Though the band stole many fine clothes from its victims over the years, Toothless preferred the rough and savage look of animal skins. Most of the hair on his head was gone, and his attempt to grow a beard produced only a few twisty yellow strands. He had not bathed in living memory, and foul odors wafted from every part of his body. With his broad back, muscled arms and savage temper, Toothless was the only one of the band who might survive a fight with Finch. But he was utterly loyal to his master and reveled in his stature as second in command.

Toothless smiled, pleased at this opportunity to do

Finch's bidding. And when he smiled, he revealed his nickname to be less than accurate: a few black-green teeth still clung to his badly diseased gums. His mouth was a constant source of excruciating pain, which only added to his violent demeanor.

"I'll be back soon enough," said Finch. He shoved the jagged knife into its sheath, slung the leather pack over his shoulder, and left to search for the child he needed to complete his quest.

Finch was a thinker, a planner. As he tromped through the forest, toward a village south of Jack's fortress, he thought again about Jack's gold and how to make it his.

Like everyone else, he'd heard the story of Jack now and again over the years. It was popular among common folk who spent the dark nights sharing tales of heroes and magic and monsters. But Finch came to notice a difference with this story. He remembered especially one old white-bearded man. By the glow of a fire, the old man told of the boy cutting down the beanstalk and the giant crashing to his doom. Then he pointed to a distant place and spoke these words: "And they say Jack is yet alive, an old man now, and he lives in a great house, with wealth beyond imagination—a house that lies somewhere north and west of here. . . ."

Of course Finch didn't believe one word about magic beans and giants. But he began to think there was a seed of truth to the story after all—the bit about a rich old man in a house full of gold. Because time and time again, a storyteller would end the tale of Jack in a similar way, even indicating the same direction: *north and west of here.*

Every so often it was necessary for Finch's band to move on to a new hunting ground. After months of murder and thievery in one area, the band grew notorious, and the locals grew wary of traveling alone and unarmed. They might even join together to hunt down Finch and his gang. But Finch always knew instinctively when they had overstayed their welcome. Then the thieves would vanish into the night, travel for miles, and find a fertile new land of unsuspecting victims.

Wherever they went, Finch would seek out the storytellers—the people who spun tales in exchange for a meal and a place to bed down for the night. One ancient woman claimed she had met a traveler who saw the house of Jack many years before, in a place between the mountains and the sea.

Finch had no map to guide him. But from the stories, he imagined he could get a fix on where Jack's house might be, if it truly existed. When the time came to move on, their words were his compass: *north and west of here.*

Many seasons had passed. Finch was certain he was drawing closer, because the storytellers added new elements to the end of the tale. *They say Jack and his mother built themselves a fortress, with great walls of handsome white stone. . . . Jack's mother passed away long ago, but Jack still lives. . . . They say Jack is generous to the poor and*

*the hungry. . . . Jack is old, and despite his wealth, is a sad man
who never leaves his house. . . .*

One day Finch learned that he was nearer to his goal
than he had imagined possible. They met a minstrel
who knew the tale. Although the man was unnerved by
the rough appearance of the gang, Finch coaxed the
story out of him with a silver coin. The minstrel had
seen the white stone house with his own eyes, and it was
only a week's journey away. An old man named Jack still
lived there with his servants. He was a sad and mysterious figure, but everyone agreed that he was rich, with an
endless supply of gold—the source of which was said to
be the magical hen that laid the golden eggs. "To find his
house, just follow this road north to the mountains, then
take the western path when you reach the crossroads.
Avoid the eastern way, for a plague has taken a village
there," the nervous minstrel told them.

Finch's dark heart thumped with glee. The only part
of the story that mattered to him was true indeed. Jack's
wealth was real. And he knew where to find it.

As for the minstrel, that was the end of his song. One
of the gang fancied his clothes, another wanted his
instrument, and Finch took back his piece of silver.

One week after that encounter, late in the day, Finch's
gang stood on a ridge at the peak of the western road. To
the north, the ridge grew taller and fatter until, some
miles off, it could be called a mountain, the first peak in
a craggy spine a hundred miles long. The western side

was illuminated with golden light, while the eastern slopes looked cool and dark. Finch could see the ocean disappear to the west. The sun was extinguishing itself on the watery horizon.

And below him, only a few miles away, was a great house of white stone. Glowing in the fading daylight, it was the brightest object on the landscape. Finch reached out, and with his thumb and forefinger, fancied that he was pinching the fortress. "Got you at last. The house of Jack."

Finch noted with pleasure that a thick forest lay between the mountains and Jack's house, creeping within an arrow's flight of the walls. A perfect place to make camp. A perfect place to observe and learn. And for two weeks, that was what he and Squint did.

They caught fleeting glimpses of the old man who must be Jack when he went to one of the high windows. One afternoon, as storm clouds filled the sky, the old man was on the rooftop, staring at the thunderheads as they rumbled by.

Jack was not alone. A young girl, no more than six years old, lived there too. There were at least four servants: three young men and one woman. Two of the men were strapping specimens who looked like they could take care of themselves in a fight. Indeed, one might be a match for Toothless John. The other man was a little older and of more ordinary proportions.

Every fourth day or so, this one would emerge from the fortress in a one-horse cart and drive off along a path that cut through the forest. The cart was always laden with a trunk or two. What was inside, Finch could not guess. Two or three days later, the driver would return to Jack's fortress.

Finch watched, waited, and planned. He was certain his twelve could overpower the old man's four, especially at night while some slept. When the front door opened, he saw how one man could easily slide the huge but well-greased bolt that locked it from the inside. The only question was how to get in, and now he had the answer to that: Find a young climber to scale the vines.

Hold it, Finch, he thought. He stopped in the middle of the forest. *You're not thinking. Where are you going now? To the farmlands near Jack's house? All you'll find there are fat, happy farm boys who won't come with you unless you snatch them. And then what? The whole county's out looking for the missing boy. No, you've got to find a kid who'll be glad to help you—a kid no one will miss, with no place else to go.*

Then Finch remembered something the doomed minstrel told him. *Avoid the eastern way, for a plague has taken a village there.*

"Where there's a plague, there's orphans," he whispered to himself. "Now you're thinking." It was risky to approach a plague-stricken village, but his instincts told him this was the way to find what he was looking for.

Besides, experience taught him that such an illness runs its course and disappears.

Finch changed directions and headed east through the forest. He thought again of the gold that would soon be his. The more he thought about it, the faster he walked. Soon he was running.

CHAPTER 3

Nick tilted his head toward the noise. Was it the leaves hushing and rustling in the breeze, or was it running water? He stepped forward and other sounds emerged: gurgling, trickling, and the crystal music of water dashing among stones. Spying a wide, shallow stream through a gap in the trees, he ran to the banks and dropped to his knees to drink from a bowl he formed with his hands.

When he finally looked up, he was surprised to see a small farm on the other side of the stream—the first hint of humanity in two days. His impulse was to hide among the trees so that he might creep back at night like a mouse for shelter and food. But a second glance revealed that the farm had been forsaken some time ago. The fence around the pasture was in disarray and no cows or horses were in the fields. The thatched roof of the one-room farmhouse was partly collapsed, and the walls of the round stone well were crumbling.

In front of the tiny house, a rusty ax was buried deep in the largest of several tree stumps. A few old pieces of wood were scattered around. Nick wondered if the farmer had simply given up on trying to draw life from this stony soil and walked away. *Or maybe,* he thought with a painful memory rising in his heart, *the sickness has come here, too. Perhaps the remains of the people who dwelt here could still be found in the house that became their tomb.*

Hopping from rock to rock, Nick crossed the stream. The farm stood in the shadow of the ridge that he'd seen from afar. Rocks were plentiful here. The farmer had used them to build low walls around his vegetable fields. But now weeds and saplings and shrubs were reclaiming the land.

A pang of hunger clawed at Nick's gut. Nobody had tended that field for years, but some vegetables might be growing wild there yet. He raced over and was clawing through the weeds, uprooting anything that looked like a carrot, turnip or onion, when he heard something from the direction of the ridge: the high *clack-click-clack* of a stone striking other rocks.

He turned and saw a man standing halfway down the slope, perfectly still. The stranger's eyes followed the tumbling stone until it came to rest at the bottom, settling among a pile of other pebbles and boulders that had rolled down over the years. A prickly chill swept over the back of Nick's neck. This man might have been creeping stealthily toward him, until one loose stone had given him away. Nick lowered himself until he was hidden among the weeds.

When he lifted his head again to peer out, he saw the stranger coming forward again. The man moved casually, with his hands thrust in his pockets. He kicked a few stones ahead of him as he descended, as if he didn't care how much clamor he made now that his presence was revealed. He reached the bottom and sauntered toward the farm. The closer he came, the more nervous Nick felt. The man was large and strong, and despite his fine clothes and his offhand demeanor, he still seemed like a predator ready to spring. There was a sheath at the stranger's waist with the handle of a knife jutting from the top. His smile didn't belong on the same face as those cold blue eyes.

Has he seen me? Nick wondered, sinking lower into the weeds. The stranger's gaze fixed on the ax in the tree stump, and he ambled toward it, whistling. He let the pack that was slung across his shoulder slip to the ground, and he gripped the handle. He gave it a little tug, then a stronger yank, but the ax would not budge. The wood had swollen since the day long ago when, with a final swing, the farmer sank his blade deep.

"Like Excalibur in its stone," the stranger said, but not to himself. He spoke loudly, projecting his voice toward the garden. It was an intelligent voice—but not a friendly voice. Nick flattened himself on the ground, wishing he'd run at the first sight of the intruder.

"Come on out, boy. I saw you from up there, you know. Besides, you're not as good at hiding as you think. I can see the path you made through the weeds."

Nick had seen rabbits freeze in place, hoping to go unnoticed when someone approached; now he felt as they must. He knew he should bolt, because this stranger radiated danger the way a bonfire threw off heat. But he thought about it a moment too long. He heard a single footstep coming toward him, and the stranger was suddenly hurtling over the wall. Nick jumped to his feet and turned to run, but powerful hands seized him from behind—one on his arm and the other grabbing a handful of hair.

"Hold on now, pup. Mister Finch won't hurt you. Unless you try to *run away*." He accentuated his words by twisting Nick's hair, so fiercely that it felt like the back of his head had caught fire. Nick stopped struggling.

"I will let go of you now," said the man. "And I want you to turn around and look at me. If you run, I'll just snatch you up again, so there's no point to it, is there? Do you understand me?" Nick nodded, and the man released his grip. Nick turned to face the stranger who called himself Finch.

Finch looked Nick over from head to toe, and he seemed to approve of what he saw. "Oh, you'll do, won't you? Can't weigh more than four stone, can you? Got twigs for arms—is there any strength in them?"

"What . . . what do you want from me?" Nick said, panting. He rubbed the arm that Finch had seized. Five bruises, one for each finger, had blossomed there.

Finch painted a broad, friendly smile on his face. "Just a little favor, that's all. Tell me your name."

"Nick."

"Nick. A fine name. Is this your farm? Is this where you live?"

Nick shook his head.

"So what are you doing here, then? Are your mother and father around?"

Again, Nick shook his head.

"What about friends? Any friends around here?"

Another shake.

"That's a shame. But you know what, Nick? I could be your friend. My name's Finch. I've been looking for a kid just like you. And here you are, in the first place I looked. That makes me think it was meant to be. You see, I need a favor that only a little fellow like you can do. A big fellow wouldn't do for this job."

Finch flashed his smile again, but Nick's fear grew nonetheless. Finch seemed to sense that his charm wasn't working, and his eyes narrowed.

"Think about it, Nick. You need me, too. I know you do. See, I understand everything about you, though I never met you before this moment.

"You lost your family somehow. Did they abandon

you? No, it was the plague, wasn't it?" Nick felt his entire body go rigid and wished he'd been able to control himself better, because Finch's eyes narrowed further and his smile spread a little wider.

"Thought so," Finch said. "The villagers probably burned down your house, without bothering to bury the dead. Then you were on your own, and there was nobody to take care of you. Maybe you asked passersby if they could give you a place to sleep, a place to come home to. But nobody ever did. Who needs a lost child like you in times like these, and a plague orphan at that? They had their own problems, their own mouths to feed. So they turned you away. The best they would do was toss you a scrap of bread. And you'd watch as the family hurried away, not looking back. And you were jealous of those children, with their full bellies and their clean faces and their little toys."

Nick clenched his teeth and pressed his lips together. *I won't let you see my face*, he thought, and he turned his back on Finch. But Finch stepped closer and whispered over his shoulder. "So you went on begging for food, wandering around, searching for a place to call home. Did a little stealing, too, didn't you? Anything to survive. And now look at you, scavenging in an old vegetable garden like an animal. But think about it, Nick: Winter will follow. And what will you do when there's no food to scrounge—you, with your cheeks sunken in and all your ribs showing already? How do you keep warm when the nights are cold enough to freeze spit, and you've got no coat to wear, no blanket to wrap around you, no fire to cozy up to?"

Nick's head bent low. His knobby shoulders were trembling.

"Nick, I was that way once too. Shunned. Hungry. Hunted. I figured I had a choice to make. And I chose to fight back, survive any way I could. You understand? I've done some wrong along the way. But the world did me a load of wrong first, and maybe I'm just paying the world back in kind."

Nick wiped his cheeks with his sleeve, and turned to look Finch angrily in the eye. Finch leaned over a little, putting his face closer to Nick's.

"Come with me, lad. I've got friends who were all just like you once. We live in a forest over that ridge. You can join us. We'll be your family. You can stay warm by our fire. And we'll feed you right—meat, biscuits, soup, you name it. How would a nice hot bowl of venison stew go down right now, Nick?"

At the suggestion of food, real meat, Nick's mouth suddenly flooded with saliva. He swallowed it before it could spill out over his lips.

"There's something you have to understand first, though, Nick. You see, we're a band of thieves. That's the plain truth. If you come with me, you'll be a thief too.

Pretty soon I'll have a little job for you to do. Nothing you can't handle. But you have to do it, and you have to do it my way. And in our band, my way is the only way. You understand? Have we a bargain, little thief?"

Finch stuck out his hand. With his eyes narrowed into slits, he stared down, and waited to see if Nick would shake it.

CHAPTER 4

"Men, meet Nick. Our littlest thief," said Finch.

Nick stood wide-eyed in the forest clearing as Finch's band gathered around and looked him over. This was the grimmest, fiercest collection of people he'd ever seen.

Some came out of their tents. One got up from a whetstone where he sharpened a deadly looking blade. A few just seemed to materialize from behind the trees. The big one with almost no teeth, giggling like a crazy man, seemed barely human; he looked like the embodiment of the evil that Nick only sensed under Finch's handsome veneer. He was considering whether he could possibly escape by sprinting into the forest when the smell hit him.

It was the smell of hot food. A thick man with a black beard was standing by the fire, stirring something inside a kettle. As the cook stared back at Nick, he brought the long-handled spoon to his nose and gave it a deep, wet snort. The spoon overflowed with steaming, meaty brown stew, dotted with yellow chunks of carrot. A few drips went off the spoon into his beard, joining the other debris that clung to the black whiskers.

Nick winced as hunger pains knifed through his midsection. His legs shook. He felt dizzy, as if he might faint.

"Smells good, Pewt," said Finch to the cook. "Make a bowl for our guest, won't you?" The man named Pewt managed to nod and scowl at the same time. Nick watched, transfixed, as the big spoon went into the kettle three, four, five times, filling a wooden bowl to the rim with the thick stew. Pewt put the bowl on a crooked wooden table, where a fallen log served as a bench, then stepped back and folded his arms. Nick took one step toward the table, but Finch's strong hand had him by the collar.

"Hold on there, lad, that stew's so hot you'll burn your tongue."

"I don't mind," said Nick. He strained against Finch's grip, never taking his eyes off the bowl.

"I won't hear of it! Tell you what, Nick. Do a little favor for me, then you can eat all you want. Show us if you can climb this tree over here." Finch pointed to one of the tallest trees in the forest, the ancient oak that marked the thieves' lair. Surely magnificent in its prime, the tree was now a knotty, rotten behemoth. Parasitic vines swarmed over its dying limbs, and black ants spat sawdust from the holes in its trunk.

Nick knew what the cruel man meant: If he didn't

climb the tree, there would be no meal. Finch released him and stood up, putting his hands on his hips. He dared Nick with his eyes to decline the challenge.

There were some chuckles from the gang, and Finch arched one eyebrow in amusement. Nick scowled and bunched his hands into fists. He wanted to pound Finch's smirking face, but he had a good idea of what would happen if he tried. So he turned his rage to the tree. With a scream, he ran right at it, leaped, and grabbed a low branch.

The branch was dead. It snapped off as Nick pulled himself up, and hit the top of his head with a *thunk*. Then his momentum carried him into the trunk of the tree. To save his nose, Nick turned his face to one side. He scraped his cheek badly on the coarse bark, before he bounced off and hit the ground.

The gang hooted with laughter. Some doubled over with mirth; some merrily slapped each other on the shoulders. The big crazy one was lying on the ground, pointing and kicking madly.

Nick held his palm to his stinging face. He looked at the tree again, plotted a safer way up using the swarming vines for grips, and began to climb. The higher he went, the less the gang laughed. He felt a rush of satisfaction as he silenced their ridicule.

Standing on a great horizontal branch, far above the gang, Nick stared down at Finch with a defiant expression. "All the way up, boy!" Finch shouted through cupped hands. Nick looked to the upper reaches of the tree. He had a problem now. The vines did not grow this high, and the only branch within easy reach appeared unsafe. Its bark had fallen off, exposing the pale dry wood underneath. Sure enough, when he tugged on the branch, it cracked off in his hands. He let it drop, giving it a careful nudge in Finch's direction as he released it. Finch glared up as the rotted branch landed inches from his feet.

With that limb gone, Nick had only one option left. The next branch was higher and farther away. He couldn't reach it without jumping. If his aim was off or his grip was weak, his life would end in a bloody crunch on the forest floor.

He heard Finch's voice from far below. "Hurry up, Nick. Stew's getting cold!"

Nick looked at the gang. Only the big toothless one was laughing now, his tongue lolling like a dog's. The others stood watchfully, probably hoping for a dreadful and spectacular ending.

Nick steadied himself with one hand on the trunk beside him, bent his knees, and launched himself. For a moment that seemed infinite, he was airborne. Then the branch slapped into his fingers. His legs swung under and beyond the branch, the force nearly making him lose his grip. As he swung back, he was able to secure his handhold. He heard voices calling from below.

"That's the way, Nick!" "Thattaboy, Nick!" Most of

the band clapped and whistled their approval.

He waited for his swinging motion to subside, then hooked his leg over the branch and pulled himself up. The rest of the climb was easy. Branches radiated like spokes from all sides, and he soon reached the top of the tree.

Nick clung to the thin trunk and swayed in the refreshing breeze that whistled over the forest canopy. The ancient oak towered over its neighbors. He looked to the west, where the sun had already set. Beyond the forest, he spied a handsome white fortress, perhaps two miles away. Then he caught the scent of the boiling stew far below him and remembered why he'd dared to climb so high.

"More, please," Nick mumbled, the last spoonful of stew bulging in one cheek. He slid the empty bowl toward Pewt, who looked at Finch. This would be the fifth helping.

"He said I could eat all I want!" Nick reminded Pewt loudly. Finch gave the cook a single sharp nod. With a heavy sigh, Pewt ladled the bowl full again. The rest of the gang waited anxiously, to see if there would be any left for them.

Nick scraped the bowl clean, then dropped the spoon and licked the insides. He slammed the bowl to the table, leaned back, and let out a deafening belch.

A full stomach was a novelty for him, and his began

to ache. Nick walked, slightly bent, to a soft place on the ground near the fire. He lay down on his side and rubbed his protesting belly. Then exhaustion overtook him. His head bobbed and his eyelids fluttered shut.

Finch watched the whole time, with narrowed eyes and a subtle smile. He told Toothless John to fetch a spare blanket and cover the boy.

When someone woke him with a whispered warning, Nick didn't know how long he'd been sleeping. One rough hand was over Nick's mouth so he could not yell. The other was across the top of his head, pinning him down so he could not turn to see who was behind him.

"Don't make a sound, Nick. If I take my hand away, you promise not to talk?"

Nick nodded as best he could in the iron grip. The man took the hand off Nick's mouth. He left the other across Nick's forehead and eyes, and went on quietly talking.

"Don't try to see who I am now. I'm just here with a quick word of advice, then I'll be off. You're a brave one, Nick. Anyone can see that. But you're just a boy, and boys do things that ain't so smart. So heed these words: Whatever you do, never, ever cross Finch. Or try to leave the band. Once you join Finch, you're his till the day you die.

"Listen to this story, lad. It's instructional. A few years back, on a late summer night just like this, one of our gang decided he could get the best of Finch. We had ourselves a bunch of fine jewels we'd stolen in our travels. Finch likes jewels, you know, because they're small and easy to cart around when we move on. One morning the bag of jewels was gone—and so was this fellow, a bloke named Montescue. As angry as you might have seen Finch get, he was a hundred times as mad when he found out one of his own betrayed him. He looked more like a demon than a man that morning, I tell you.

"He stood there for a while, thinking dark thoughts. Then he gathered up a few things in a pack. He told us he was going on a little trip, and we should stay where we were until the next full moon, then move to a new forest he'd scouted. And then he turned and walked off. I don't know how he knew what direction to go. Finch just has a sense about those things—lets his instincts guide him, like a wolf.

"The full moon passed, and we saw nothing of Finch. We moved on like he said, with that crazy Toothless John in charge. Autumn came, autumn went. We started to think he'd never be back.

"One night, after a storm that left every tree covered with snow and ice, we were all gathered close around the fire to keep warm. Then we heard a horse coming, clop-clop, through the woods. I looked around, and everybody was shaking—and it wasn't from the cold. Who'd be out riding on a bitter night like that? The sound got closer and closer, until at last the horse and the rider came out of the blackness and into the clearing.

"I thought I was looking at Finch's ghost. Nobody else said a word, so I guess they had the same idea. Even Toothless was cringing. The horse was all white and bony, and Finch didn't look much better. He got down, moving all stiff and slow, and walked over to our circle around the fire. The fellows on that side scooted out of his way.

"Finch walked right up and practically put his nose into the flames. I could see that his whiteness was from the snow and ice that stuck to his clothes and hair. He stood there a while, just melting. Then he reached into his coat and brought out that old bag of jewels. The sack had dark stains all over it now. He looked every one of us in the eye as he held it, then he let it drop to the ground. Next he reached deeper into his coat and drew out that knife of his. Even from where I sat, I could see all the notches and dents in the blade.

"Finch threw the knife into the ground between his feet. 'Sharpen that,' he said. Nobody moved for a second, but then Toothless grabbed the knife and ran for the whetstone. Finch sat by the fire and stared at the flames. Not a minute later, he just keeled over, asleep before he hit the ground. He slept all night, and the day after, too. That bag just lay next to him the whole time. Nobody dared to touch it, or look inside to see if all the jewels were still there.

"We never got the whole story from Finch about how far he ventured to catch up with poor Monty. But the point is this: If you betray Finch, he'll follow you to the ends of the earth for revenge. Finch never forgives. Never forgets. You get what I'm telling you, lad?"

Nick nodded.

"That's good. I'm leaving now. Don't try to see who I am. Understand?"

"Yes. I won't," whispered Nick. The hand came off of Nick's eyes. He heard footsteps fading away. When he finally dared to look around, he saw no one, and all the tents were dark.

CHAPTER 5

Nick was still sleeping when Finch grabbed a handful of his shirt and pulled him to his feet. His legs wobbled for a moment as he snapped out of his slumber.

"Morning, boy!" said Finch. Nick's dark hair was a tangled mess. Finch spat on the palm of his hand and smoothed it down. "Now that you've slept on it a bit, tell me: Are you glad you joined this band of mine?"

Nick looked around, wiping grains out of his sleepy eyes. Most of the gang was awake already, and some were staring at him. He remembered the warning from the night before, and looked at their faces, but couldn't guess which one had come to him in the night. It took a while to decide that the incident had really happened and he had not only dreamed it. Suddenly he realized that Finch was waiting for an answer. He knew there was only one safe reply.

"Yes, I'm glad," he half mumbled.

"Happy to hear it," said Finch. "But I wonder if you

have the grit to be a thief like the rest of us."

Nick straightened out of his slouch. Hadn't he proved himself by climbing the tree? "I'm a thief already, you know."

"Truly, now? And what have you stolen?"

"Food, mostly. Other stuff, too." Nick shrugged. He wished he hadn't left his sack of trinkets behind when he was chased from the farm.

Finch smirked at him. "You'll be stealing more than food for me, Nick. Are you thief enough to get away with it?"

"I am."

"We'll see."

The entire band hid on opposite sides of the forest road. Finch didn't hear the approaching wheels yet, but his sharp ears caught the whispered conversation between Squint and Pewt.

"What kind of a nutty robbery is this?" muttered Pewt. "Why don't we just drop a tree across the forest road and put an arrow in the driver's back when he stops?"

"Finch knows we can do it that way," Squint said knowingly. "But that's not the point. The point is to test the kid's character, and make sure he hasn't got any."

Pewt snorted. "When is the wagon coming, anyway?"

"Should be any moment now. I spotted them at Jack's fortress, loading the chest onto it first thing this morning."

Finch had heard enough. "Quiet over there!" One day

soon, that nettlesome Pewt was going to wear out his welcome. Finch was thinking about ways to end the cook's employment when he heard the sound he was waiting for.

Nick was a hundred yards down the road, closer to the approaching wagon. Holding a long coiled rope that was tied to a large iron hook, he crouched behind a tree that grew by the roadside. The other end was knotted securely to a knobby root of the tree. He could hear the wagon drawing near but would not be able to see it until it rounded a bend in the road, just ahead of where he hid. His nerves were jangling as he went over Finch's instructions in his mind.

The volume of clattering hooves jumped as the wagon drew near the bend. Nick poked his head out and risked a quick look. The horse came around first, a handsome brown beast pulling the wagon briskly along. Before the driver came into view, Nick pressed himself against the side of the tree.

Finch had instructed him well. As the wagon rolled by, Nick kept his back to the tree and circled around, always out of the driver's sight. Then, with the hook in hand, he ran after the wagon, staying as low and quiet as he could. The rope uncoiled as he ran.

Nick kept his eyes on the driver's back, afraid the man would turn and see him. But the driver was unsuspecting, whistling as he rode through the cool, sun-speckled forest.

Nick was fast and nimble, and he soon caught up. This was the most dangerous moment: mounting the back of the wagon, without alerting the driver. "If you just jump right on, he might feel your weight jostle the wagon," Finch had told him. Finch seemed to be an authority on all things nefarious. "So wait until the wagon runs over a bump, or hits a rut, and then climb aboard. That way, he'll never notice."

Sure enough, one of the wheels hit a stone. As the wagon bounced, Nick grabbed one side and hauled himself aboard. He looked up, certain the driver would turn around and catch him, but the man just chuckled at the rough ride and resumed his merry whistling.

The wagon had walls on both sides but no gate in the back, to make it easier to slide cargo in and out. The chest was right in front of Nick, a wide wooden rectangle with metal and leather hinges. Nick had to hurry now. At any moment, the rope would pay out completely. Creeping forward on hands and knees, just a few feet from the driver, he put the hook over the near handle of the chest. Then he retreated, glad to be beyond the man's reach. He swung his legs over the back of the wagon, slid off, and ran to hide behind a thick shrub. As he turned to watch the results, Nick was surprised to find himself exhilarated by what he'd just done.

The rope snapped taut, forming a long, straight line between the root of the tree and the back of the wagon. It twanged like the string of an instrument. As the horse trotted on, the chest slid off the wagon bed and fell with a heavy crash.

The driver whipped his head around. When he saw the chest lying in the road behind him, his mouth dropped open in a dumbfounded expression. Nick had to clap a hand over his mouth to stifle a giggle.

The driver tried to shout something, but could only sputter. Then he pulled back on the horse's reins, and the wagon came to a stop. He stood on the bench and looked back at the trunk. It dawned on him too late that someone was up to no good. His head swiveled like a storm-blown weathervane as he saw twelve dangerous-looking men burst from hiding and charge from every direction. As Nick watched the savage attack, he suddenly found the situation not funny at all.

The driver fumbled for the reins to spur his horse on, but two men seized the horse's bridle. Toothless John leaped on the cart and drove a hammering fist into the driver's jaw. The poor fellow dropped headfirst to the ground. The gang surrounded him, each one bearing a club, a knife, or an ax.

The driver struggled to his knees, holding his head and grimacing with pain. Then he looked at the merciless bunch around him and his face went pale. He tried to talk, but his voice trembled as he pleaded for mercy.

"Look, boys, I won't give you any fight. Take it, you can have the chest. The horse and the cart, too. Just let me go, won't you? Please?" Finch laughed first and the rest of the gang echoed him. They drew their circle tighter, like a noose. The driver put his hands together, either begging or praying.

Nick stepped from his hiding place and ran closer to see what would happen. Finch stepped forward and grabbed the sobbing driver by the hair. He raised the jagged knife with his other hand.

"No!" screamed Nick. Finch froze, then turned his head slowly around. He held the blade high and glared at Nick for a long, long moment. Then he tucked the jagged knife into its sheath.

"Don't worry, lad. We're just teasing him a little. That's all." Finch pulled the driver to his feet by the hair and gave him a shove toward the wagon.

"Go ahead, my friend. On your way. We will keep the chest, as you were so kind to offer."

The driver gaped at Finch, his breath hitching. He turned to go, but the gang still surrounded him in an unbroken circle.

"Let him go!" Finch growled. Toothless stepped aside at once. With an exaggerated, mocking bow, he gestured for the driver to pass. The man took a hesitant step, then ran for the wagon. Toothless John stuck his foot out and tripped the driver as he ran past. The man stumbled into the side of the wagon. With a whimper, he climbed onto the bench, snapped the reins, and urged the horse on.

Some of the gang looked puzzled. Some looked angry. Pewt stared after the wagon, shaking his head.

Finch ignored them and gave Nick that mask of a smile. "Nicely done, Nick. Why don't you go open that chest and see what we've got?"

While the boy ran to the chest, the gang turned to Finch.

"What was that all about?" hissed Pewt. "Since when are you so merciful?"

"Shut up, you maggot," shot back Finch, talking low so Nick would not hear. "Are you blind? Did you see the look on that boy's face? He's got no stomach for blood. He might have run off on us, and that would have spoiled everything. Listen, all of you. This was just a test, to make sure he'll do as we say. We need him for one more job, and that's that. You can do whatever you want with him after he gets us into Jack's house." Toothless John looked pleased at the thought.

"Aren't you forgetting something, Finch?" asked Squint. That little smirk was back on his face.

Finch whirled around angrily. "What?"

"The advantage of surprise. Lost it, haven't we?"

"What are you talking about?"

"Well, what do you suppose will happen when that wagon gets back to Old Man Jack's place, and the driver tells Jack what a lovely time we showed him in the forest? Don't you suppose they'll be a touch more concerned about defending the fortress, with a band like ours lurking about?"

As Squint's words sunk in, Finch closed his eyes,

bared his teeth, and pounded his palm with a fist. He felt like he might explode. Squint took a step back, perhaps thinking he'd tweaked his volatile leader too much.

Then, just as suddenly, Finch calmed himself. He let out a deep breath, opened his eyes and began to speak softly. The gang passed quick glances to each other; they always found his icy composure more unnerving than his rage.

"No, we haven't lost anything. We simply have to move our plans up a bit. That fellow was heading away from Jack's house. He won't be back till tomorrow, if he has the courage to come back at all. And we'll attack *tonight*." Finch had waited too long for this opportunity. He would not be denied.

"Hey!" the boy yelled from down the road. "The chest is locked—it won't open!"

The band strutted over. Finch squatted beside the chest and inspected the lock for a moment, twirling his arrowhead beard. He pulled a slender pick from his pocket. "A fool could pop this lock. Squint, I'll have this open before you can finish 'Tom's Gone.'"

Squint cleared his throat and recited:

> Tom's in the farmyard
> To steal himself an egg;
> Along comes the farmer
> And cuts off his leg.
> Tom's gone a-hunting
> On the King's royal land;

Along comes the sheriff
And cuts off his hand.
Tom's gone a-napping
In the Queen's royal bed;
Along comes Her Highness
And—

"Got it," said Finch. The lock clicked open and Finch swung the lid up. He looked inside, and then he put his boot against the chest and kicked it over in disgust. "Bah! Nothing but books!"

Books spilled onto the dirty road. It was a heap of worthless junk to the gang—too heavy to haul on their journeys, and besides, there wasn't a scholar among them. But the boy seemed enthralled. He picked up the most colorful book from the pile.

"You know how to read, boy?"

"Just some letters. I never got as far as words."

The boy flipped through the pages with an unpracticed hand. Inside on every page, there was a single large letter, a drawing, and a word underneath: *A* with a picture of an ax. *B* with a picture of a bee. He turned several pages together. There, with the letter *G* was a picture of a giant.

"You like that book, Nick? It's yours, for a job neatly done," said Finch. "The rest will kindle our fires. Let's get back to camp."

Two of them tossed the books back into the chest and picked it up, sharing the load. The band went back into the forest, heading for their lair, and Nick followed with the book tucked under his arm.

Finch walked nearby, observing. He'd come close to losing the boy. But Nick seemed more at ease now—even a little proud of his performance, and pleased with his reward. Finch was sure the boy could be trusted with one more task—the only one that mattered.

All Nick had to do was climb the vines and open the door to Jack's house. The less he knew about that beanstalk nonsense, the better. Finch didn't want crazy ideas getting into the boy's head. And as for what would happen after the door was open, the boy must know nothing of that at all.

Finch pictured the small group of people who lived in Jack's house: the servants, the little girl, the old legend himself. Reaching to his side, he gave his jagged knife a gentle squeeze.

He looked forward to meeting Jack and his friends, very soon indeed.

CHAPTER 6

Things were busy at the encampment that afternoon. Some of the gang sharpened their blades and axes. Others threw knives at targets stuffed with straw.

As night fell, the air turned unusually cold, raising the prospect of a killing frost weeks before its time. The moon appeared, nearly full, bringing crisp illumination to the world below.

Nick was wearing different clothes now, pants and a shirt of much finer material. Squint, who had some talent for tailoring, had cut and sewn stolen clothes down to size for him. They were dyed black so Nick could approach the fortress unseen. The shirt even had a cowl sewn onto the back that Nick could pull over his head to further conceal his presence.

Compared to the rough and itchy texture of Nick's old tunic, this softly woven fabric felt like heaven. It had pockets, a novelty for him. On this cold night it felt good to bury his hands deep inside them.

When Nick shed his old garment to try on the new, Squint took one sniff and tossed it into the fire. Nick watched it burn. The whole time he was on his own, eking out a bleak existence, he wore the same rag. Now it was going up in flames, and the smoke curled and sifted through the trees. Then it was gone altogether.

Later Nick sat by that same fire, stroking his throat with one hand. He couldn't get the image out of his head: Finch standing over the helpless driver.

"Something the matter, boy?" Again Finch had crept up silently behind him. "Not having second thoughts, are you? I'm counting on you, you know."

Nick saw cold eyes staring back, icy blue hoops around black holes. It was frightening, the knack Finch had for guessing what he was thinking. Nick recalled the anonymous warning and chose his words carefully. "I'm not having second thoughts. I'll do what you want."

Finch paused for a while, cracking his knuckles and looking wary. Then he sat and leaned close. "Listen, Nick. What we're doing isn't wrong, the way I see it. When you see a falcon swoop down on a rabbit, do you blame the falcon for what he's done?"

"No."

"Of course you don't. Because that's what falcons do. They take what they need to survive. It's no different with people, Nick. You're either a rabbit or a falcon in this world. Remember when I found you in that field, squatting down to nibble on some vegetables? You even looked like a rabbit, frightened and weak, waiting for someone to pounce. Lucky for you I came along. Now you're one of the falcons, one of the strong—all because I took you under my wing."

Finch peered at Nick's face, trying to judge the effect of his words. Nick fought to keep his expression unreadable. Finch gripped Nick's shoulder, and his fingers dug in like talons.

"Just don't disappoint me, boy. Here, tell me the plan again, so I know you've got it straight."

"I wait until you tell me to go," Nick recited. "Then I run to the fortress. Climb up the ivy to a window. Get inside and go downstairs. Look for the big door and slide open the bolt that locks it shut. Then push the door open just a crack, come outside, and signal you with the lantern."

Finch nodded his approval. They sat and watched the fire for some time, both lost in their own thoughts, before Nick spoke again.

"Finch," said Nick, "do you think Old Man Jack really has a hen that lays golden eggs?"

Finch stiffened. "Who told you about that?"

"Squint told me, while he was sewing these clothes for me. He said the fellow we're stealing from is supposed to be the Jack that climbed the beanstalk."

Finch glared at Squint, who was sitting under the great oak, scratching his fleas with both hands. "And did our friend Squint tell you the whole story?"

"No, I already knew it. Everyone knows it. But it's just a story, isn't it? There aren't really giants and beanstalks and magic hens."

"That's right. Just a story. Now get some rest."

Nick went to the other side of the fire, where he'd slept the night before. He lay on the soft mossy ground and pulled the blanket over himself. He was anxious about the task ahead, and it was difficult to sleep. So he did what he often did when sleep would not come easily: He tried to remember his mother's face.

There was a time when he could remember her clearly, and his father, too. But as time passed, a dark haze settled across those memories.

As Nick closed his eyes and concentrated, he could see the shapes of their faces, but the features shifted and blurred, never quite right, never truly resolving themselves into the mother and father he had known.

There must be something wrong inside his head, Nick decided. The images he did not want to see—Finch, the knife, the driver's throat—he couldn't banish. And the things he truly wanted to remember slipped away the harder he tried.

Hours later Nick stood by the forest's edge, flanked by Finch and Squint. Except for one thug that Finch dispatched to a position north of there, the rest of the gang was gathered in silence behind them.

The moon was still high, throwing too much light,

but Finch had no choice—this would be the night. Beyond the woods, Nick saw Jack's fortress on the low hill. The sentry paced along the top of the near wall, then turned the corner and disappeared from sight.

Nick had caught only a glimpse of the fortress when he climbed the dying oak to earn his dinner. Now that he saw the place in its entirety for the first time, he marveled over the pristine walls of white stone.

Finch knelt to issue final instructions. "When you go in the window, look for the stairs to the lower level. The front door will be down there, on the opposite side from where you enter. When you slide the bolt and open the door, turn left and come around the corner to face us, then give us the signal. Understand?"

"I know what to do," said Nick.

"Smart lad," said Finch. He stepped to the edge of the clearing and lifted the covered lantern, which now had a long cord tied to its top. Keeping it hidden from the fortress with his body, he opened and closed its hinged door three times. A moment later, a lone figure emerged from the forest. With a bow in one hand and a slain deer slung across his shoulders, he might have been an innocent hunter who stayed out late and was heading home. The sentry soon spotted him, and went to the corner of the fortress to watch the stranger amble past.

Finch handed Nick the covered lantern and slapped him on the back. "Now, Nick. Run!" With the black cowl pulled over his head, Nick raced into the open field and up the gently rising slope. Dressed in black from head to foot, he looked like a shadow that had escaped its owner and gone fugitive.

It wasn't a long way, but to Nick it seemed like a mile. The fortress grew closer with agonizing slowness. It was like running in a dream.

At last he reached the safety of the walls. The only way for the sentry to see him now was to stick his head over the side and look straight down.

Nick pulled the cowl back and tilted his head to look at the soaring walls. He'd never seen a building this tall; the fortress seemed to go up forever. The window he had to enter was just a dark slit high above, flat across the bottom and rounded at the top. Against the white stone, the ivy looked like veins filled with black blood.

Now that he was standing here, looking at the vines that seemed dangerously thin and weak, the task seemed hopeless. But there was no turning back. The hard look in Finch's eyes had made that clear.

Nick needed both hands to climb, so he took the free end of the cord that was tied to the lantern and knotted it to the belt around his waist. He reached out and grabbed two of the thickest vines, one in each hand, and pulled himself up, choosing his first foothold where two vines intersected. The ivy held. He repeated the motion, shifting his weight smoothly from hand to hand, foot to foot. As he rose, the lantern was a pendulum beneath him, swaying gently at the end of the cord.

Moving steadily, Nick was soon halfway up the wall. *Maybe I can do this.* He paused for a moment when he heard the sentry walking above him. He knew the man was unlikely to see him, but he held his breath anyway, until the footsteps moved off.

Another minute brought him a few feet from the window, where a stone sill jutted a few inches out. The vines grew thinner here, and Nick sensed them loosening as he climbed. *Careful now.* A single jerky motion might cause the ivy to lose its grip on the rock and send him plummeting.

Nick's foot slipped off a toehold, putting all his weight suddenly on the vines in each hand. He probed frantically with his feet for support. As the vines in his hands peeled away from the wall, he began to topple.

In desperation, Nick reached for a seam between two of the great stones. Just before he lost his balance completely, his fingers slid into the crack and he steadied himself.

Before he could sigh with relief, he heard below him a clang of metal hitting stone. He looked down in horror. His near fall had started the lantern swinging wildly. It had struck the wall once, and after bouncing off, was coming back to hit it again. In Nick's precarious position, he could not move to prevent it.

But this time, the lantern hit the soft leaves of ivy instead of the stone, and the sound was muffled.

Nick looked up, expecting the sentry's head to appear over the top of the wall. He heard footsteps approaching. But the man simply walked by, just as before, unaware. Nick allowed himself to exhale, then climbed the remaining few feet.

He was just below the window, ready to reach over the sill, when a loud scream pierced the silence. It came from inside the window. Nick was so startled he nearly echoed the scream. The rapid footsteps of the sentry approached, not ten feet above. He yanked the cowl over his head and pressed himself against the wall.

"Little Ann, are you all right in there?" the sentry's voice called down. Nick was sure he'd be seen clinging to the vines, only half hidden by the jutting sill.

The sound of a young girl crying came from the room. She was calling for her father. Nick heard a door opening, and the voice of an old man.

"Ann, my little love, what is it? Have you had a nightmare?" The little girl went on crying, unable to speak.

"There, there, now. Remember, your daddy's gone off in the wagon, and he won't be back for two days. But Jack is here to take care of you," said the old man.

That's him—that's Jack, thought Nick. *And the girl's father—that was the man we robbed in the forest this morning.*

"Is everything well down there, Master Jack?" called the sentry. Nick shut his eyes, as if that would help him stay hidden. He heard Jack come to the window. The old man leaned out to speak to the sentry on the wall above. The hand resting on the sill was inches from Nick's shoulder.

"It's fine, Bill. Just a nightmare. Too many scary stories from wicked old Jack, I'm afraid."

The sentry chuckled. "Yes, sir. Poor Ann. Too bad Henry's not here." The sentry resumed his watch. Jack held his hand out in the night air.

"Who would think it would grow so cold after such a fine day? Ann, you should close these at night. Here, I'll do it." The old man pulled the heavy curtains from either side and they met in the middle.

Nick was dizzy with relief. If Jack glanced down, he'd have been seen for sure. And as the sentry looked over the wall, Nick must have blended into the shadows below the windowsill. He gave silent thanks to Squint for the black garments.

Nick waited while Jack calmed the little girl. There was something haunting and familiar about the way the old man spoke to the child. It wasn't that Nick knew Jack's voice. It was that some time ago, his parents spoke to him that way, in soft and comforting tones. They were voices that went with the faces he could no longer remember.

"Tell me, Ann. What were you dreaming about?"

The crying had stopped, but the girl's voice trembled. "The giant was chasing me."

"Oh, my!" said Jack playfully. "I guess I shouldn't tell you that scary story anymore."

"No, I like to hear it!" Ann said excitedly, her mood shifting abruptly.

"Oh, you do, now? What part do you like best?"

"I liked it when the giant chased you. But why couldn't he catch you, Master Jack?"

"What's that you say?"

"If the giant was so big, why couldn't he run faster than you or climb down the beanstalk faster?"

"Hmmm. I guess young Jack was too quick for that bad old giant. Or maybe the giant was afraid of heights!"

"But then how did you chop the beanstalk down so easily? You were just a boy, and you said the beanstalk was bigger than a bunch of trees."

"What, you doubt my strength? Feel that muscle!"

The little girl giggled. "But what happened to the giant when he fell and died? What did you do with his bones?"

Despite his growing misery from the cold, Nick was interested in Jack's answers. The girl asked good questions.

"My stars, what a curious child! That last one will take a little explaining, I suppose," said Jack. He whispered as if revealing a fabulous secret. "You see, little Ann, that beanstalk was a mighty thirsty plant. Imagine how much water a plant would need to grow so big! The roots of that beanstalk spread all around like this. . . ."

Nick heard the little girl laughing hysterically. Jack must have been tickling her.

"And they sucked all the water out of the ground.

That made the earth very dry and dusty. When that wicked giant came crashing down, he made a deep hole in the ground, and a great cloud of dust and dirt and rocks flew into the sky. And when the air finally cleared, there was no sign of the giant. But the beanstalk—that you could see for months before it rotted away."

"But Master Jack, why did—"

"So many questions!" interrupted the old man, laughing. "I'll answer one more, and then you must promise to go to sleep."

Yes, please go to sleep! thought Nick. The strength in his hands was failing. And though he'd found a good handhold in the stone, it felt as if the vines under his feet were weakening.

"Master Jack?"

"Yes, my love."

"Isn't it wrong to steal?"

"Yes, it is wrong."

"But didn't you steal those treasures from the giant?"

The old man didn't answer for a while. Then, in a different, sadder voice, he said, "Yes. I certainly did."

"But was it all right, because the giant was evil?"

"What do you think? Is there ever a time when it's right to steal?"

"I don't know."

"Well, you do something for me, Ann. Think about

that as you fall asleep tonight. And in the morning, you tell me what you've decided."

"Yes, Master Jack."

Nick heard the door close inside that room. Now that Jack was gone, he had to hold on as long as he could to give the girl a chance to fall asleep. But the muscles in his arms and legs were on fire, while the cold stone was numbing his fingers and toes.

A minute passed, maybe two. He didn't know if the girl was sleeping yet, but he couldn't wait another second. He wasn't even sure if he had the strength to climb into the window anymore.

Jack kissed Ann good night, then stepped into the hall outside her room and eased the door shut. His smile faded and his shoulders slumped as the familiar feeling overtook him. He felt like a drowning man who came to the surface only briefly to feel the sun shining on his face, and then despair gripped him again as it always had and tugged him into the dark abyss. He was an old man, but he suddenly felt even older.

"Why did she have to bring that up?" he muttered. "For a few moments, I had almost forgotten."

It occurred to him that the golden candlestick in his hand was worth more than every object in the miserable cottage where he'd grown up. *Look at me now, though*, he thought. *As rich as a king.* Because of what he'd brought down long ago.

All his, all stolen. *But somebody paid for it, didn't she? Probably with her life. And that's the part of the story that nobody tells.*

How was he supposed to explain all that to the little girl behind the door? He put the candle on the table outside Ann's door and shuffled to his room, praying that a dreamless sleep would come quickly for once.

● CHAPTER 7 ●

Finch was in a frenzy, shifting his weight from foot to foot as he waited for something—anything—to happen. First, the boy had nearly fallen. Then a child's high scream, barely audible, came floating across the field, and he was sure Nick had been nabbed. But no, the sentry left and now the boy hung there under the window. They could just make out his shape in the moonlight. *So close!*

"Squint, what the devil is he doing?"

Squint peered intently at the dark form below the window. "He's still waiting there—no, he's moving now. He's going in!"

Finch froze, afraid he might hear another scream. The corner of one eye began to twitch. Seconds passed and no sound came from the window.

"He's done it," Finch said. Beside him, Toothless John laughed and rubbed his hands together. Finch turned to face the band. "Now, remember the plan. Inside, we split into two teams. I'll take one upstairs, Toothless and the

59

other stay below. We'll leave the sentry on the roof for last. When you find servants, get rid of them quickly, before they can scream and alert the rest. But remember: Leave the old man for me to deal with. There may be hidden booty that only he can lead us to." Finch poked the rough skin of his palm, testing the sharpness of his jagged knife.

"If everyone does his part, this is the night that makes us rich. No mistakes!"

Nick crouched on the floor just under the window. He breathed through his mouth to keep his labored breath from hissing through his nose. He flexed his cold, aching fingers. The girl never moved, so he was sure she was asleep. He picked up the lantern, tiptoed across the room, opened the door a crack, and slipped into the hallway.

He closed the door slowly, praying its hinges would not squeak. It slid silently into its frame, and he relaxed for a moment. The difficult part was behind him now. *Finding the front door should be easy.*

Nick undid the knot that tied the lamp to his belt, so he would not trip over the rope as he crept through the dark. He looked down the deserted hallway. It ran the length of the fortress. In the center, a wide staircase descended to the lower level.

Nearby on a wooden table, a tall candle burned in a golden candlestick. Another stood at the far end of the hall, just a flickering yellow star from this distance. Nick ran his hand over the ornate curves of the candlestick and onto the surface of the table. It was beautifully crafted, with inlaid designs of precious metals decorating its surface.

There was a strange, soft sensation under his feet. Looking down, he saw a carpet that ran the length of the hallway—the first he'd ever stood on. It was dark green and blue, with a pattern that looked something like twisting vines. Threads of gold were woven throughout, glimmering in the candlelight.

Nick gulped. Around him were objects of greater value than he'd seen in his entire life. The house must be filled with such treasures. What could be the source of so much wealth?

Nick knew he should head straight down the staircase and slide the bolt on the front door. The gang would be expecting his signal any moment now. But a question popped into his mind: *What if it really happened?*

It seemed impossible. But there was something about the way the old man answered the girl's questions, something in his voice. Nick had heard storytellers before. They liked to act as if the story they were telling was real, even though it was just a story. But Jack's voice was different, as if he was trying to act as if it was just a story, to hide that fact that it was *real*.

Nick's thoughts were spinning. Was he crazy to think like this?

And something else troubled him. What exactly would Finch's gang do to the people in this fortress when they got inside? They had been ready to kill the wagon driver in the forest, the man who must be the girl's father. Would they hurt Ann, who couldn't be more than five years old? Would they murder Jack?

Nick realized with sudden clarity what a fix he'd gotten himself into. If he opened that door for Finch, death would visit this place. He had to think of something else, a plan of his own. And he realized what he really wanted to do: He wanted to find out if the story of the beanstalk was true.

He decided to explore the fortress to discover the answer. And when he learned the truth, he would grab the most valuable objects he could carry and sneak out a window on the other side, where the gang wouldn't see him. Then he would run far, far away, where Finch would never find him.

Nick wondered where to go first. On the side of the hallway where Ann's room was, all the doors looked alike. Nick supposed they were bedrooms too.

But on the other side, to the right and left of the staircase, stood two pairs of wider, taller doors. Nick walked softly to the nearest pair and pulled on a handle. Despite the massive weight of the ten-foot-high door, it opened easily.

It was dark, but Nick sensed a large open space before

him. There were windows, but the moon was shining on the other side of the fortress, and its light did not penetrate here. Nick stepped inside and gently shut the door behind him. Then he raised his lantern and opened the hinged side to let out a shaft of light.

Nick clamped his hand over his mouth to cut off his own scream. There, towering over him, was a horrible giant, with gleaming red eyes, mouth twisted in a ferocious snarl, and hands reaching down to grasp with long pointy fingers.

But a second glance told him the giant wasn't real. It was only a painting.

What a painting, though! No wonder he was fooled at first glance. The walls in the room were as high as two men, and this work of art reached almost from floor to ceiling. The giant was rendered with incredible skill and obsessive detail. Every wart, every hair, every blemish on the skin received the artist's attention. The background, too, was astonishingly real. The giant stood by a great kitchen table with whole tree trunks for legs. A chair was lying on its side, toppled over when the monster leaped to his feet. The eyes glowed with a wicked inner light, and the way it seemed to be reaching right off the canvas made Nick shiver.

Nick raised the lantern over his head and gazed down the length of the room. The walls were crammed with pictures, too many to count. He knew who the artist must be. And sure enough, in a bottom corner of the picture before him, he saw the painting signed with a single letter:

J

Nick walked along the gallery, casting the lantern's light on Old Man Jack's amazing pictures one by one. Each depicted moments from the famous story, together telling almost the whole tale. There was the mysterious stranger—what strange green eyes he had!—trading the beans for the cow. There was the beanstalk towering in the morning sky, with the little boy Jack gazing up, astonished.

In the next picture, Jack climbed the beanstalk at a dizzying height, as the countryside shrank away beneath him.

Another painting showed the top of the beanstalk reaching the mysterious cloud where the giant lived. This was a landscape from a dream, a rocky coastline with frothing mist beating its shore instead of ocean waves. It was an island in the air, held aloft by some unseen force.

In another picture, a giantess stood at the door of the giant's castle, looming tall over little Jack. She had a pleasant face, compared to the vicious portrait of the giant Nick had seen first. Her black hair was neatly combed back and tied with a ribbon. Nick was surprised by an unexpected detail of this picture: Her belly was huge and round like a ball, and she cradled it with one hand while she spoke to Jack. With the other hand, she pointed back down the path the boy had taken. Her mouth formed an O, and Nick imagined her saying, "Go! Go away! If my husband catches you . . ."

At the far end of the room, Nick saw the back of a large easel, holding another canvas. Drop cloths were spread beneath it to protect the floor from splattered paint. As Nick drew closer he caught the scent of oils. He walked around to the other side to see what the old man was painting now.

This one had just been started. Some of it, in fact, was still a charcoal outline. It showed young Jack, wielding an ax, hacking away at the bottom of the beanstalk. Through a wondrous use of perspective, the point of view was from Jack's feet, looking up the length of the beanstalk. The giant was high above, barely visible. The mighty growth had already begun to topple.

The leaves of the beanstalk glistened in the lamplight as if wet with dew. Nick touched that spot and his fingertip came away green.

All those paintings, Nick thought, must have taken a lifetime to produce. And now it seemed the old man had reached the end of the story. But why did he paint with such devotion? Was it because everything that came after his grand adventure seemed so humdrum in comparison? Did he spend his life trying to relive it in this gallery?

But that answer didn't feel right to Nick. If these paintings were created to celebrate those events, why was it that the lingering impression they left was of despair? There was something about the somber shadows in every picture, and the joyless look in the eyes of every subject. Jack himself looked especially haunted.

Nick realized that he was no longer questioning whether the story was true. The art around him made it hard to believe otherwise.

Standing before the easel, Nick had come almost to the end of the room. He turned around to see what was left to discover.

There, against the far wall, was one more picture: a portrait of the hen that laid the golden eggs. It was a huge bird, three times the size of an earthly hen, in a nest that sat upon a pedestal. She was asleep, with her head tucked under a wing. Nick walked toward that last painting, holding the lantern before him. The background image was the beanstalk rising into the blue sky. It framed the hen prettily.

With every step forward, Nick grew more amazed at how lifelike she looked. Every fiber of every feather was so perfect. It seemed you could touch them. Several of the plump golden eggs sat around the hen in the nest, and they actually sparkled in the lantern light, their shadows dancing as the flame flickered.

But how could the shadows move? Nick wondered—and then he realized that only the beanstalk in the background was a painting. The pedestal and the nest and the hen and the golden eggs were *real*.

Nick stopped, hardly able to breathe. He put the lantern on the floor. Reaching out carefully so he would not disturb the sleeping bird, he put his hand around one of the eggs and lifted it. It seemed to be made of solid gold, and it was far heavier than he expected. But it resembled a regular egg in every other way, down to the tiny pores in the shell.

He wouldn't find anything more valuable than this. He took another egg and stuffed one in each pocket. They were so weighty he didn't dare to carry more, or the pockets could rip loose.

There were windows on each side of the nest. He tiptoed over and looked out of one. This was the opposite side from where Finch and his band were hiding. Vines grew here as well, and they looked as sturdy as the ones he'd already climbed.

Even the sharp-eyed Squint wouldn't see him if he left this way. With luck, he could be miles away before Finch knew he was gone. Despite the warning he received the night before, Nick was sure Finch could never find him. How would he even know where to look?

Nick draped a leg over the windowsill, but then he stopped to think.

Why not steal the hen?

He looked at the bird. There was the ultimate prize, the endless source of wealth that spawned all the splendor around him, even the fortress itself. It would not be long before the golden eggs in his pockets were spent and gone. But if he made off with the hen, then one day he'd be as wealthy as Jack himself. It was the permanent solution to his poverty.

Nick returned to the easel and picked up the smallest drop cloth. It was made of a thick fabric, so he thought it might adequately muffle the squawk of the hen. He could throw the cloth over the bird, pull the edges together and carry it like a sack. Then he would be out the window, down the wall and into the woods in a minute, running where neither Jack nor Finch would find him. Yes, it was risky, but imagine if he succeeded!

He held the cloth up with both hands and walked lightly toward the bird. When he was close enough, he tossed the cloth over its body and scooped it up.

The bird did not wake. Nor did it move. He uncovered the hen to look closer. He was holding a dry, stuffed animal forever frozen in that sleeping pose.

"It died thirty years ago, boy," said a voice from the other end of the room. Nick snapped his head around to look. Jack was standing at the door. The little girl from the bedroom was behind him, peeking around the old man's side. And a powerful-looking young man, one of Jack's guards, was halfway down the gallery, charging fast.

With a shout, Nick tossed the hen in the air over the man's head. The startled guard skidded to a stop and caught the bird. Nick used that moment to run for the nearest window. He jumped for the opening, but he'd forgotten the heavy eggs in his pockets and fell short.

Before he could scramble completely out, the man grabbed him by the heels and hauled him in, kicking and struggling.

Jack walked slowly down the long room with the little girl tagging along. As the old man walked, he used a candle to light a series of torches on the walls. Soon the room was filled with their flickering glow.

Nick gave up resisting. He stared at the floor with his chest hitching as the guard reached into his pockets for the eggs, and handed them to the old man.

Jack stood before Nick. He wore a robe of shimmering silver cloth embroidered with gold. With his gray hair and long beard, he looked like a wizard.

"That's the trouble with stolen goods, boy," said Jack, hefting one egg in each hand. "They're always more of a burden than you expect." Jack turned to the young girl behind him. "Thank you, Ann. Why don't you go back to bed now."

The girl didn't reply. Nick had the feeling she was looking at him. He looked up and met her accusing stare. Her expression made him blush with guilt.

"I wasn't sleeping, you know!" she called.

"Faker!" It was the only reply Nick could think of. The man holding him started to laugh, but quickly stifled it.

"Why did you steal from us?" she asked angrily.

"Because I've got nothing, and you've got everything!"

"That doesn't make it right!"

"But it's right for me to starve?"

The girl didn't know how to respond to that. She just said "Humph!" and stormed away. Jack watched her go, then bent to pick up the stuffed hen that the guard had placed on the floor. He brushed the ruffled feathers, put it back in the nest, and returned the eggs to the hen's side. He spoke as he arranged the objects.

"She lived a long, long time, as hens go. But I guess even magic birds don't live forever. I had her preserved so I could always remember her."

Jack turned to look Nick in the eye. It was a penetrating, unsettling stare. "She's full of sawdust now. Do you know what the man said was inside that bird when he opened her up?"

Nick shook his head.

"Nothing. Nothing out of the ordinary, that is. She was just like a regular hen. So how, I wondered, could she lay eggs of solid gold?" The old man paused, letting Nick think about it.

"And I could never figure it out. But people are like that too, you know. If you were to cut them open, you couldn't tell one man's guts and bones from another's. But some people produce wondrous things from what's inside. And some of us are thieves."

"It *is* true," whispered Nick. "The story. You and the beanstalk."

Jack looked at Nick for a long time. A new expression came to the old man's face, as if he recognized something familiar in the little thief before him. Nick saw lines of sadness in that face that looked as if they were engraved a long, long time before.

"What's your name?" Jack asked.

"Nick," he answered quietly.

"What's the rest of it?"

"That's all. Just Nick."

"Tell me then, Nick. How did you get in here?"

"Up the vines." Nick didn't see any reason to lie.

"So you climbed up here. A poor little boy. To steal my treasure," Jack said. Even Nick understood how those words echoed another story from so many years before.

The old man kept staring, nodding his head. He seemed to be making a decision. Then he did something totally unexpected.

"Thank you, Roland," he said to the man who had captured Nick. "That will be all for tonight."

Roland looked at Jack with raised eyebrows. "You want me to leave?"

"Yes. You may go," said Jack.

Roland opened his mouth to protest, but saw the serious look on the old man's face. "Yes, Master Jack. I'll be awake if you need me."

"Thank you, Roland."

Roland walked to the door and took one last worried look back at his master.

"Close the door, please, Roland," said Jack. The door swung shut, and only Nick and the old man were left in the gallery.

The old man bent to whisper to the young thief. "Are you alone?"

Nick swallowed hard over a lump in his throat. "Yes," he said, and as the words came out he knew they were true. He wasn't going back to Finch and the band of thieves. He was on his own.

"It's not just my gold you're after, is it?" said Jack, stepping closer.

"No," Nick said, mouthing the word more than speaking it aloud.

"What, then?"

"I wanted to know. . . ."

Jack's eyes, wrinkled all around, narrowed until they were nearly closed. "And what if it was true, Nick the Thief? What if you had been me, sitting there?" He pointed at a painting of himself as a boy, sitting as if knocked to the ground, and staring at the awesome beanstalk that towered into the heavens. "Would you have climbed it? Would you have dared?"

There was a long silence. Nick stared at the painting, wondering, *Would I?* And he could feel the old man's gaze upon him.

Jack stepped toward the painting and slid his hand behind one side of the gilded frame. *I could run for the window right now,* Nick thought. The old man was making it easy to escape. But now, Nick realized, he needed to know the truth.

There was the click of a latch, then Jack swung the entire painting away from the wall like a door, revealing a dark space behind it.

Without a word, Jack stepped into that darkness. His candle shed a shrinking rectangle of light around him as he moved through a hidden passageway. Nick followed, putting a hand out to each wall to guide him. The walls were cool and wet at his fingertips. Before him, the old man abruptly turned to the right and disappeared. When Nick reached the corner, he saw Jack standing in a small chamber.

There was a harp leaning against one wall. Large and luminous, it seemed to be made of some material that was half glass and half gold. On one side, its frame was in the shape of a lovely woman with diamond eyes.

"When I first brought her down, Nick, she would sing for you. You just had to ask. Or you could look in her eyes and *want* her to sing, and it would happen. The music went into your heart, and it was so beautiful you could never describe it.

"But she doesn't sing anymore. Hasn't for many years. In time, her magic—her life—just faded away, like the hen's."

Jack was quiet for a while. Then he spoke again. "But the harp is not what I brought you here to see."

There was also a plain wooden table in that room, with a simple box resting on it. The old man put the candle beside the box and removed the lid.

Nick wasn't close enough to see the bottom, so he stepped forward. Inside was a leather pouch. The old man turned the pouch upside down, and three beans spilled out into the box, milky green in color. He laid the pouch on the table.

"This is why I brought you. Watch them," said Jack. He blew out the candle. Immediately Nick could see a faint green light emanating from the beans. The sight amazed and confused him. If Jack used his beans long ago to grow the magic beanstalk, where did these come from?

"It was the night after the beanstalk fell," said the old man, anticipating Nick's question. "A single stem grew from where the plant had been rooted. It just came up, right before my eyes. Within a minute, it had a flower, and then a pod. These seeds were inside the pod. Until this moment, nobody else in the world knew about them but me."

"Can I touch one?" asked Nick. Jack did not reply. Nick picked up a bean and held it close to his eye. It glowed from within. It looked like a tiny point of green starlight was inside, with even tinier points of light circling it, and even tinier points circling those.

"Why does it glow like that?" asked Nick. Again, the old man did not reply. "Hello?" said Nick. He turned around and reached into the darkness where the old man was just standing. *Jack was gone.*

Nick was afraid. Without the candle, the only things he could see were those beans. One glimmered in his hand, and the other two stared at him from the box like a pair of cat's eyes. He picked them up and held all three in his palm. They seemed to glow a little brighter together. Nick even thought he could feel a strange energy, a sort of tingle, passing into his palm and through his wrist.

Nick groped for the pouch on the table and found it. Holding the beans in front of him, using their meager glow to light the way, he made his way carefully out of the room. Once he turned the corner into the passageway, the light from the gallery made the going easier. He half expected to be seized when he entered the big room, but it was deserted. The old man was nowhere in sight.

"You want me to steal them, don't you?" he said aloud. Once again no answer came. Nick stuffed the beans into the pouch and put the long loop of cord around his neck.

"I will then, you crazy old fool!" He climbed onto the ledge of the window, took one last look for the old man in the gallery, and vanished into the night.

Jack stepped out from the shadows of the passageway. In the darkness, the boy had walked right by him.

"Am I mad?" he asked aloud. *Letting the boy walk out like that?* Of course he was. But the burden was growing every day. And just when it seemed he would be crushed at last under its weight, the little thief appeared.

How strange it was, to meet this boy. Like flying back through time and meeting himself.

But no, not himself—not exactly. There was more to this one, something different. You could see it in his eyes when you looked past the desperation and fear.

"Go on, boy," he said. "Go up." *And I will wait for you below. So you can tell me what you've seen. And then I'll know at last.*

What became of her.

● CHAPTER 8 ●

Finch twisted the point of his knife into the bark of a tree. "What the devil is keeping that brat? We should be inside by now!"

"Having trouble with the door, maybe. Or he's caught," said Squint.

"Shut up and keep your eyes on that fortress," muttered Finch, stabbing at the tree.

"I'm only trying to—" Squint broke off in the middle of his response. "Someone is coming through the woods."

Metal sang as the entire band brandished their swords and daggers. They stood poised to attack as the footsteps grew louder and then relaxed as a familiar figure came into view. It was Marlowe, the one Finch sent to distract the sentry.

"He's run off!" Marlowe said, panting.

Finch grabbed Marlowe by the front of the shirt and shook him. "The boy? You mean Nick?"

Marlowe nodded and continued, watching the knife

in Finch's hand. "I did as you told me, Finch. Then I was on my way here when I saw him run across the field. You couldn't have seen him from this spot, but I did. I tried to catch him but the little bugger was too quick. By the time I got to where he went into the forest, there was no sign of him."

With a snarl, Finch shoved Marlowe into a tree. Marlowe fell to the ground in a painful heap. Nobody stepped forward to help him up.

Finch tucked the knife away and put both hands to his face, trying to think. His plan, his dream, was disintegrating—because of that boy. When he lowered his hands, his jaw was shaking.

"He's betrayed me." The words barely escaped through Finch's clenched teeth. "He found a prize in Jack's fortress and wants it for himself. But we'll find him. And we'll make him sorry."

"He . . . he went east, through the forest," Marlowe said meekly, still lying on the ground.

"East. That's a start." Finch closed his eyes and tried to let his instincts guide him as they had so well before. *If I were that little rat, where would I run?*

Nick stood on top of the ridge. Below him was the abandoned farm where he first met Finch. It had taken a while to find it again, but he was here at last, only a few minutes before sunrise.

Moving carefully, he went down the slope, grateful for

the growing light of dawn, and reached the bottom without slipping on the loose stones. He walked to the center of the farm and sat on the stump beside the buried ax to rest.

Nick pulled the leather pouch from inside his shirt, leaving the strap looped around his neck. He poked two fingers into the mouth of the pouch and pried it open. Turning the pouch over, he let the three beans tumble into his open palm. He brought his hand up to his face to examine them more carefully. Now that they were out in the daylight, even this weak morning light, their glow was no longer visible. He covered the palm with his other hand, forming a dark cave for the beans, and peeked inside between his thumbs. Once again, he saw those shimmering green lights.

"What are you?" he asked aloud.

For a long while, Nick just sat and watched them. Was it really possible that these three simple beans could create an awesome ladder to another world?

And where was that other world, that island in the clouds? He looked at the sky. Only a few wisps of clouds were visible; otherwise it was just the daybreak's gentle gradation of color, from the deep blue of night to the blushing pink that heralded the sun.

Unlike Jack so many years ago, Nick knew what was supposed to happen when the seeds were planted. It would be so easy to just drop them on the ground to let them grow. But at the same time, he was afraid to let it happen. All the strange events of the last few days had simply swept him along. Choices were presented to him, by Finch and Jack. Each man, in his own way, seemed to look into his soul. Finch saw a little thief who would open the door to Jack's treasure. Jack saw a little thief who would steal these beans and call forth the beanstalk again.

The beans. They were the reason Nick had come to this remote spot, far away from villages and prying eyes. It was a farm, after all—a place to grow things.

He looked around, clutching the beans in his small fist. The overgrown vegetable field seemed like the right place to plant them, so he hopped over the rock wall. He dropped to his knees and, with his free hand, ripped weeds away to expose a patch of bare soil.

"Nothing to be afraid of," Nick told himself. He held his breath. Opening his fist, he turned his hand sideways. The beans stuck to his sweaty palm. With the fingers of his other hand, he prodded them loose. One, two, three beans dropped to the ground. Nick watched closely, afraid to breathe. Nothing happened, and at last he exhaled.

"Am I doing this right?" He rearranged the beans into a neat triangle and sat back to watch again. Nothing happened. He began to feel foolish for believing in their power. Maybe the old man was playing a joke on him.

"No, you're real, all right. I know you are." He pressed his thumb deep into the soil beside each bean and pushed them into the holes. Then he scooped a handful of loose dirt and filled each cavity. Brushing the rest of the soil off his hands, he squatted next to the spot to see what would happen. This felt right, but something was missing.

"Water. Bet you need water." The old stone well was there, but any bucket and rope were long gone, so Nick ran to the stream and scooped up water in his cupped hands. He walked back gingerly, trying not to spill, and poured a little over each hole. It didn't seem like enough. An old rain barrel at one corner of the house held some stale water, but it was too heavy to carry. Nick wondered if there was a smaller container of some kind in the farmhouse. He trotted toward the dark doorway.

Just before he stepped inside, he saw a metal object glint as it caught a beam of morning light that penetrated the shadowy house. He stumbled back as a figure inside the house stepped forward. It was Finch. His face was the distillation of pure rage, his teeth bared in a snarl, his eyes wild. Nick yelped like a puppy and turned to run. When he spun around, he was looking at Toothless John.

He darted to one side of the vile man. Toothless John reached out and caught hold of the leather pouch around his neck and snapped it back. Nick was yanked off his feet, the strap cutting into his flesh. He fell with a rough thump on his back. Before he could move, Finch was standing over him, reaching down with one strong hand. In the other hand he held his jagged knife.

Finch's hand clamped around Nick's neck and lifted him until his feet dangled a foot from the ground. Nick grabbed Finch's wrist with both hands to keep himself from being strangled. The rest of the band emerged from the broken-down farmhouse and gathered around. Finch held his blade to Nick's face, the jagged edge pressed against one cheek. His jaw was clenched so tight, he could barely spit out words.

"Didn't you know, boy? Didn't you know what I would do to you?" Then, abruptly, Finch wasn't looking at Nick anymore. He was looking down at his own legs.

Nick followed Finch's gaze. Finch's body, from the waist down, was covered with ants. And not only that, but the ground was swarming with living creatures. A thousand more insects scrambled through the weeds. Dozens of blind black moles emerged from their tunnels and fled. Beetles unhinged their shells and took flight. A rabbit bolted in a blur. Hidden birds exploded from the grass and bushes. Countless worms were writhing out of the earth, as if the soil had been poisoned.

Finch uttered an "Ugh!" of disgust. Throwing Nick aside, he tried to swipe the bugs off with both hands.

Nick was on the ground, gasping for air on his hands and knees. As he caught his breath, he became aware of an odd sensation: Wherever he touched the ground, there was a *tingling*. The feeling grew. It passed through his palms. It flowed past his wrists, almost to his elbows. Goosebumps erupted all over his body.

Toothless John was screaming and stomping and swatting his face with his hands. A swarm of wasps had flown from their underground hive and were angrily stinging him. The thug ran away howling. The rest of the band scattered in a panic, leaving only Finch and Nick at the farmhouse.

Now the crawling bugs found Nick, and they began to climb his arms and legs to escape the strange tingling. Nick wiped them away and jumped atop a boulder. He looked over and saw that Finch had stopped trying to brush off the ants, even though they were up to his chest, his neck, his face, even climbing in and out of his gaping mouth. He was staring goggle-eyed at something behind Nick.

And then Nick could *hear* what Finch saw. He turned around, not sure he really wanted to know what it was.

The ground there was heaving, and the tingling sensation was joined by a deep rumbling sound that resonated in his chest. A high dome of earth arose where the seeds were sown. It heaved up and down, as if a giant heart beat fitfully at its center. And spreading out in all directions from the center of the mound, it looked like a dozen creatures were burrowing outward, pushing the grass up as they tunneled along.

Finch snapped out of his trance as one of the burrowing things came right at him. He opened his mouth to scream, but Nick couldn't hear anything above the rumbling. Then Finch ran off into the woods, faster than Nick had seen any man run.

Another burrowing thing was coming right at Nick. It went directly under the boulder he was on, knocking it right out of the soil and sending Nick tumbling. Nick leaped to his feet. The subterranean thing suddenly broke through the earth and shot ten feet in the air. It towered over Nick's head, green and glowing like a firefly, as thick as a post, and twisting and coiling like a serpent.

A snake! Nick thought. *A giant worm!* But it was neither, he realized. This was no animal; it was the root of a plant—the root of the beanstalk. But no plant ever moved like this. Nick ran to the farmhouse, clumsy with fear, and hid behind the rain barrel at the corner. Behind him, the root paused, reared up, and then suddenly plunged forward again in Nick's direction, diving back into the earth.

Then it came up again, several feet ahead. It arched up and over and down again, then up and down again, always toward where Nick was hiding. At the edge of Nick's wide-eyed vision, he saw other roots plunging in and out of the ground, sewing giant green stitches in the earth, and he knew they were searching for something. They were *thirsty*, and the world trembled as their circumference grew.

The root was upon Nick's hiding place now, paused and hovering over the barrel. Nick watched as the tip of the root wrinkled and wagged, as if sniffing the air. Then, before his eyes, another wonder: Tendrils sprang from the root, growing in an instant, a foot long, two feet long, a yard long. They whipped around the barrel and lifted it into the air. Now there was no place to hide.

But the root found what it wanted, and it wasn't Nick. It was the rainwater. The tip dove into the barrel. There was a giant gulp, then a slurping sound as it sucked out the last drops of moisture. The barrel crashed to the ground, dry as toast, as the tendrils uncoiled from it. An egg-shaped lump was sliding down the root, toward the pulsating mound where the seeds were sewn, moving and pausing to the beat, sloshing as it stopped and started. It was water being pumped to the seeds.

In those incredible moments, Nick registered every detail of what was happening around him. A root paused at the top of the well, then slithered inside. Another root nearby, sensing some silent signal, followed it down. The rock walls of the well tumbled apart as the roots doubled in size, then doubled again, guzzling and pumping great gulps of water. Under Nick's feet, there was a tumbling, grumbling sensation as the roots probed deeper and deeper, pushing dirt and boulders aside and splitting bedrock.

Suddenly the mound gave a giant heave upward. The grass dome burst like a pimple on the earth's cheek, dirt and pebbles rained everywhere, and there was the beanstalk. No, not one stalk—*three*, rising and twining together. They shot thirty feet high in an instant, curving at the top like a trio of vipers ready to strike. Then with an unearthly roar, they pointed straight up and grew into the sky, intertwining as they rose. A living rope, thick as the greatest trees, was weaving itself before Nick's eyes, impossibly fast, impossibly long, impossibly high.

Up. Up. And up it went, gaining speed. A giant root intercepted the stream that ran nearby, dividing at its tip again and again until thousands of tiny squirming wormy fingers drank every drop. Downstream, fish suddenly flopped in the muck.

Up. Up. And up. The high grass along the garden wall, green and lush one minute, dried and frizzled into hay the next.

Up. Up. And up. A row of trees toppled as one.

Up. Up. Up so high, Nick lost his balance and fell as he strained to follow the beanstalk's path with his eyes.

He lay flat on his back, the easier to watch it go skyward. His body quivered as the earth rumbled underneath it. Nothing could tear his gaze away from the beanstalk.

Until he saw the cloud.

The cloud came from the west, from somewhere over the ocean. It appeared at almost the same instant that the sun emerged over the opposite horizon. The first rays struck the edge of the cloud, gilding it. Beyond that, all was black and gray. The cloud was gigantic, of unimaginable size and mass, like the greatest storm ever known. As it swept over the land, rapidly approaching the growing beanstalk, it eclipsed the heavens and brought the dark of night back to the world beneath it.

There was a bond between the beanstalk and the cloud. One belonged to the other, of that Nick was sure.

At the foot of the beanstalk, the plant rustled and hissed as hundreds of branches and leaves and tendrils sprouted everywhere, filling the trunk with lush green growth. The quaking of the earth had subsided and the noise had dimmed, but he could still hear the slosh of water being pumped up to sustain the growth at the top.

High above him the beanstalk narrowed to a thread in the sky, then vanished altogether, too far away to see.

The cloud was drawing closer. It had a lazy spin as it approached. But that spinning motion came to a halt and even reversed itself a bit as one part of the cloud—a narrow peninsula that jutted out much farther than the rest—aligned itself with the beanstalk like the point of a compass.

Then the beanstalk lurched skyward, straining at the roots that must have been anchored a hundred feet below ground. It seemed to be trying to stretch itself just a few feet higher, reaching for something to latch onto at the top. At the same time, the cloud itself descended to meet the rising plant.

Nick felt like a fish watching a giant ship moor itself to its anchor line above him. A rumbling noise came down as the prow of the cloud and the plant touched. A shudder ran down the length of the beanstalk, top to bottom, resonating in the earth.

And a matching shiver ran down Nick's spine.

CHAPTER 9

As Nick stood gawking at the beanstalk, a violent gust of wind swept over the crest of the ridge, down the slope, and across the valley, sending loose stones rolling and spiriting fallen leaves into the sky. This wave of air followed the strange cloud like the wake of a great sea-going vessel. As it washed over him, it made his clothes billow and snap, and he had to lean against the gale to stay on his feet. The leaves of the beanstalk rustled and whistled. Then the howling passed by, and Nick watched as the gust rolled across the rest of the valley and into the hills beyond, its strength ebbing now that the cloud had come to a stop.

Nick was a dozen yards away from the beanstalk. He approached it cautiously. As he took a step, he kicked something with his foot. It was a knife, dropped by one of the fleeing thugs. It was the kind with a blade that folded into its handle. Nick tucked it into his pocket.

Cautiously, he put his hands out and touched the

trunk with both palms. There was that tingling again, though not to the degree that drove the insects out of the ground. It was an invigorating feeling, a power that could somehow be absorbed. To touch it was to feel energized.

He spread his arms wide and hugged the trunk, putting an ear to its surface. It sounded like there was a river surging deep inside.

Nick took another look at the earth beneath his feet, wondering if he would ever touch it again should he leave. He was afraid to begin the climb, but more afraid not to. Finch and his gang of cutthroats were driven off, but would they stay away for long?

Something else helped him overcome his fear: the thrilling, siren call of adventure. Above him, on top of that cloud, was a place where perhaps only one other human being had ever set foot—a magical place, with marvels to be discovered, and maybe treasures to be retrieved.

"Jack did it. So can you," Nick said to himself.

Nick grabbed one branch and stepped onto another. Then he took a deep breath and started to climb.

He was surprised at how easy it was. Places for his hands and feet were everywhere. He never seemed to tire—in fact he felt stronger the higher he climbed— and he knew there was something unnatural about this endurance. It was the awesome life force that flowed inside the magic beanstalk, radiating through his body and fueling his muscles. His arms grabbed and pulled, his legs climbed and pushed, with endless speed and agility. Nick felt he could almost fly. Any doubt that he could reach that strange cloud overhead evaporated, like the morning mist that the rising sun was burning away.

Already the earth had shrunken away below him. *I'm a thousand feet high*, he thought, and a thrill shot from his head to his toes. He dared to let go of the beanstalk with one hand. Leaning over the void, he thrust his fist into the air and let out a long yell of sheer exhilaration.

He felt something close around his ankle. The shout of joy became a shriek of fear.

On the branch where his foot rested, a thin green tendril had sprouted and gently wrapped itself around his leg. With a little kick, Nick easily freed himself. He breathed a long sigh of relief. It didn't seem like the tendril was dangerous; it was more likely a side effect of the beanstalk's final stages of growth, as each of its stems reinforced itself by twining around the others.

Nick continued his journey upward. He paused only briefly along the way to take in the mind-boggling scenery below. He saw Jack's house, now just a cube of sugar on a green carpet. He saw the mountains to the north. Everything shrank except the ocean, which grew bigger and bluer the higher he went.

Above him, a tiny black shape spiraled slowly down, circling the beanstalk. It was a crow. The bird looked at Nick with one glittering eye and let out a caw as it reached his level. Then it flew past on its corkscrew descent, never flapping its wings, just riding the currents of air.

The birds and me, Nick thought. *The only ones who can cross between the two lands.* He continued onward, upward. The beanstalk was half as wide as it was at its foot, and still tapering.

Now the cloud island was near. Nick looked at its vast underside, which ended somewhere beyond the horizon. With its boiling black underbelly, it resembled a massive storm cloud. Nick could even see flashes of lightning here and there. But there was a difference between this and any other great storm cloud, a difference anyone would notice if they observed it carefully. While true clouds constantly change in shape as the winds blow around them, this one held its basic form.

The peninsula where the beanstalk met the cloud island was just over Nick's head now. The island was thin at this point, no more than a few yards deep, while it grew hundreds of feet thick at its interior. With his heart pounding, Nick climbed the last few yards.

At the top, the beanstalk had anchored itself to a boulder of incredible size. Tendrils gripped the stone like a many-fingered hand. Nick climbed onto the boulder. He reluctantly let go of the beanstalk; he was going to miss the energy it gave him. All about him, and apparently around the whole perimeter of this land, thick fog swept in and out like foaming ocean waves. Farther inland the fog faded until it disappeared completely after a hundred yards or so, revealing the solid ground underneath. Beyond that a rocky ridge that ran along the coast obscured the rest of the island from view.

A massive island in the sky, disguised as a cloud, held aloft by some unexplainable magic—there was no understanding it, or comprehending it, so Nick just accepted what his eyes told him.

Below his feet, under the huge boulder, he saw only fog. Nick wondered where *cloud* ended and *land* began. He slid inch by inch down the side of the boulder and let one foot drop into the mist. Finally, when the vapor was chest-high, he felt rock under his toes. He brought the other foot down next to it.

Nick shuffled toward dry land, afraid to lift his feet as he stepped, not trusting the ground he could not see. His caution paid off, as one probing foot discovered the edge of a hole that was cloaked by the mist. He reached down and found a rock, and dropped it into the opening. He never heard the rock hit bottom. The silence was chilling.

Nick dropped to his hands and knees and crawled around the wide gap, nearly twenty feet across. Then he made his way to the visible shore. As he went forward, the mist gradually cleared until it was gone completely.

He was surprised to find sand under his feet. With its sandy shore and foamy waves of vapor and rocky coast, this place resembled an earthly island in many ways.

Nick climbed the jumble of rocks, knowing he was about to get his first look at the land that Jack visited so many years before. When he reached the highest point, he was not surprised to see a gigantic castle in the distance. But he was amazed by the vast landscape spread before him.

"This isn't an island," he said. "It's a *world*."

He always pictured the castle as the solitary, dominant feature of the cloud island. But there was so much more: forests, hills, valleys, lakes, and streams. A desert sprawled beyond those, and after the desert, a craggy, foreboding mountain rose in the distance. Nick could not tell what lay beyond that. But he guessed there was at least as much on the other side of the mountain, if not more, than on the side he could see.

It had not occurred to Nick that there might be other choices, other places to explore. But he felt that the right thing to do was to follow Jack's footsteps. Besides, it was the logical place for a thief to explore. The giant died long ago, and his wife must be gone by now as well. They must have left other treasures behind that Nick could claim for his own.

Now that he was on top of the cloud island, the sun was shining on him again, climbing high as mid-morning approached. The radiance felt good beating on his back. Then something blotted out the sun. Nick turned to see a thick white cloud drifting toward him. From a distance it looked like a solid mass of white. He knew it was just an ordinary cloud, vaporous and insubstantial, but he half-expected a loud crash when it met the cloud island.

It struck the narrow edge and divided, half engulfing the land above and half disappearing below. It poured over and around Nick, feeling cool and wet on his skin. He sat on a rock to wait for the fog to pass. A few minutes later the tail of the cloud swept by and Nick could see again. He watched it depart, driven by the light breeze, unveiling once again the features of the land before him.

A forest spanned the distance between Nick and the castle. A few swirls of vapor were snagged among the trees but soon evaporated. Nick climbed down from the rocks and went into the woods.

The trees were like the oaks and maples of earthly forests. But growing among them Nick saw long, thick vines that looked like smaller versions of the beanstalk, with the same strange milky green color. Some of them snarled together in clumps; others snaked up the trunks of the trees. They seemed to be native to this place.

Is that why the beanstalk grows? Nick wondered. *Is it trying to get back where it belongs?*

Nick went on, heading for the giant's castle. The trees and undergrowth were full of chirping birds and rustling animals that he heard but never saw. Raucous crows were everywhere, flapping overhead, strutting across the forest floor, and staring from the high branches with glassy black eyes.

Nick came to a fallen tree that blocked his path. He

ran at it and vaulted, landing neatly on his feet on the other side.

A loud snort came from his right. An animal that was bigger than four oxen strapped together was digging with its snout at the roots of the fallen tree, just a few yards away. Bristly black hair stood on end across the shoulders and down the back. A head that was almost as large as the rest of the body rose from the ground, and its eyes fixed on him. It was a monstrous wild boar. Twin yellow tusks, each as tall as Nick, curled along the sides of its mouth. The beast sneezed, and dirty snot spewed from the end of its long shovel nose.

Nick froze, hoping the creature would ignore him. A wild boar was an ornery thing when disturbed, and this one was many times bigger than any earthly variety. It regarded him for a long moment, turning its face sideways to stare with one bloodshot eye. Then it lowered its head, drew its lips back in a snarl, and charged with surprising speed.

Instead of turning to run, Nick leaped to one side and rolled to avoid the onrush. The boar snapped its head at him as it passed. The tusks whistled over Nick's head.

Nick got up and ran as the boar skidded and turned to follow, its hooves churning up clumps of turf. He dashed by a stand of trees that grew in a row, creating a natural barrier. The boar followed on the opposite side, catching up in seconds. As it ran, it searched for a gap in the trees to break through and gore him. Nick looked ahead and saw with alarm that such a clearing was just ahead. He stopped himself short against the last tree in the row. His lungs were burning. The chase was exhausting him, and he longed for the energizing force that sustained his long climb up the beanstalk.

The boar came around the tree and lunged at him. Nick circled back, keeping the trunk between him and the beast. The boar reversed direction and came grunting around the other side, arching its neck to wrap around the trunk and reach its prey. It tried to crush him by slamming its tusks against the tree, slashing deep scars in the bark with every miss. Nick retreated farther around the tree and found himself dangerously close to the boar's back hooves.

The boar began to run in a tight circle, scraping its head against the bark, drawing closer with each step. Nick would be dead in seconds if he stayed. He pushed off the tree and darted through some thick bushes nearby, scrambling over and under their tangled branches.

The boar came snorting behind, uprooting the bushes with its tusks as fast as Nick could climb through them. Nick came out the other side with the beast so close behind he felt its steamy breath on his neck.

Just ahead a thick cluster of trees grew, and Nick thought he might find safety in the middle. Before he could reach it, one of the swinging tusks brushed his back, knocking him off balance. He ran stumbling for a few steps, then hit the ground.

He tumbled to one side, just avoiding the impaling tusk as it drove into the ground beside him. He was looking right into that awful pink eye. He punched at it, but the leathery eyelid closed and blocked his fist. The boar pulled its tusk out of the ground and brought its gnawing teeth toward his face.

Nick heard a snapping sound, and then the beast squealed with pain and fear. Its foreleg was caught in the metal jaws of a trap that sprang from under a blanket of fallen leaves. The metal jaws suddenly twisted halfway around, and the leg bone broke with a violent crack.

From overhead, Nick heard the clatter and squeak of ropes and pulleys. A heavy spiked contraption was descending from the trees. Wailing like a frightened piglet, the boar tried to run, but its broken leg was held fast. Nick scrambled backward out of harm's way. The deadly spikes came down hard and fast, piercing the boar through the back, the shoulder, the neck. It shrieked for the last time, then collapsed. The huge head fell toward Nick, and one of the tusks struck him hard on the skull.

Nick writhed on the ground, holding his head. The world tilted and spun in front of his eyes. His ears rang, but he was dimly aware of another squeak of moving ropes over his head. A red flag emerged from a hole in the ground and rose up the side of the tree—triggered, Nick realized, by the same clever contraption that killed the boar. He saw a stone counterweight coming down from the treetop as the flag went up, and then his vision blurred beyond perception.

That flag is a signal, he thought before everything faded away. *Someone will be coming.* . . .

❂ CHAPTER 10 ❂

Old Man Jack had not slept much. He stared out his window most of the night, wondering what would result from his impulsive decision to let Nick escape with the beans.

He felt groggy as he wandered downstairs, still in his sleeping robe. The little girl was alone in the dining hall, nibbling on a piece of toasted bread with honey. Whenever Jack saw her, the same thought crossed his mind: How sad that she'd lost her mother the year before, and how fortunate that she had a father as fine as gentle Henry.

"Miss your dad, Ann?" he asked, taking the chair opposite her. She nodded without looking.

"He should be home by tomorrow morning," Jack said. "And think how happy those children will be when they get those fine books."

Jack's servant Mary brought a plate of bread and a mug of ale to the table. It was the first thing she did for him every morning. He thanked her, and she returned to the kitchen.

Something else was on the little girl's mind. "Master Jack, what happened to the boy you caught in your painting room last night?"

"Ah, the little thief. I sent him away."

"Did you punish him first?"

"No."

"But why not? Didn't you want to teach him a lesson?"

The old man took a long sip from his mug. "Maybe it's better if he learns it for himself."

Ann scrunched her face, which she always did when she was confused. Then her expression brightened and she changed the subject.

"I thought about it, like you said!"

"Eh? Thought about what?"

"If it was all right for you to steal from the giant."

"Oh, that. And what do you think?" Jack watched the girl's face carefully.

"Well, the giant was awful and he didn't deserve those treasures. But you're a good man, so I think it was all right for you to take them." She beamed at Jack.

The old man hung his head. Somehow, he had to make the girl understand.

She reached out and put her hand on his arm. "What's wrong, Master Jack? Why are you sad all the time?"

Jack kept his head down. A chill swept through him, and he pushed the mug away and clasped his hands.

"Ann, imagine a little boy who lifts something very heavy and puts it on his shoulders. And for the rest of his life, wherever he goes, that burden is always with him. He grows to be a young man, then a grown man, then an old man, and all the while it's there. And the older he gets, the wearier he becomes, until he can barely stand to carry it anymore.

"I'm sad because I have a burden like that, Ann. But it's the kind of burden you can't see. You just feel it."

Ann's eyes brimmed with tears. "Did I give the wrong answer?"

Jack sighed. "It's complicated. Let's talk about that."

Another voice interrupted them. "Master Jack!" It was Henry, standing at the kitchen entrance.

"Father!" Ann ran over to Henry, and he scooped her up and hugged her tightly. He held his daughter for a while, rocking from side to side, before putting her down and brushing his hand through her hair, tucking it behind her ear on one side.

"Run along now, Annie," Henry said, trying to sound cheery but failing. "Father has to talk to Master Jack. I'll find you in a moment."

Jack waited for Ann to leave before speaking. "Henry, what happened? You're as pale as the moon. Why are you back so quickly?"

Henry could scarcely get the words out as emotion overcame him. "Thieves . . . on the forest road . . . thought they were going to murder me . . . lost the books . . .

afraid to come back that way . . . rode all the way around the forest to get back and warn you. . . ."

"Calm down, Henry. Sit at the table," Jack said. He called to the kitchen. "Mary, fetch an ale for Henry!"

Jack coaxed the story from his servant. He was sure the boy in the forest whose intervention had saved Henry's life must be Nick. Was that child really a member of the cutthroat gang Henry described? Then what was he up to last night? Had he entered the fortress to let the others in?

"Daddy?" Ann was at the door again.

"Darling, I told you I have to talk to Master Jack. You mustn't interrupt."

"But you have to come see the big cloud."

"Ann—" Henry stood to reprimand the child, but stopped when he saw Jack bolt out of his chair and stride to the girl.

"What sort of cloud?" asked Jack. His knees cracked as he knelt to hold the girl by her shoulders.

"A big black scary one. Come to the roof and I'll show you."

Moments later they stood on the roof. The oppressive cloud hung like a dark ceiling over most of the visible world. Rivers of lightning crackled across its belly.

"You haven't changed," Jack whispered.

Ann was bouncing on her toes. "See how big and dark it is? There's going to be a storm! I know it! Father, can we stay and watch?"

"What on earth . . ." Henry said. He was looking east, where the cloud ended.

"What? Tell me what you see, right now!" Jack demanded with sudden urgency, grabbing Henry's arm. "My sight is not as keen as yours!"

"Beyond the forest, over the ridge . . . it looks like . . . it can't be . . . it's a thin green line, reaching from the ground to the cloud. But what is that thing? It's almost like the beanstalk from your st—" Henry looked at Jack. "From your story."

Jack looked back at his servant, nodding. "Tell Bill and Roland to load the cart and prepare fresh horses. I want you to come with us as well, if you're up to it. And all of you should be armed," he said, thinking about the ruffians who had intercepted Henry.

Henry's eyebrows arched high. He was twenty-six years old, the son of a servant, and he had lived with Jack his entire life. Never once had he seen the old man venture outside the fortress walls.

"Master Jack, what's happening?" Ann asked. She stood with her hands on the top of the wall, a gentle breeze rippling through her white robe and her black hair. She gazed dreamily at the magical thread of green in the distance.

Jack thought for a while before answering. "A long time ago a boy climbed a beanstalk, and he came down a thief. Now a thief is climbing a beanstalk. And who knows what will come down?"

● CHAPTER 11 ●

Nick woke slowly, dimly aware of growing tremors. He felt them in the ground before he heard them. At first he couldn't distinguish it from the ache that pounded inside his head, but the sound grew stronger and louder. It was the steady thump of weighty footsteps. Then he remembered the flag, the signal to whoever built the trap that killed the boar. He looked over at the dead beast. A pair of crows stood on its bristly back, pecking at the ragged wounds. They heard the footsteps too and hopped into flight.

He sat up and it made him so dizzy he almost passed out again.

Through the trees, he caught a glimpse of the thing that was rapidly approaching. Low-branches hid its upper body from sight, but Nick saw two great striding legs and massive feet coming down with impacts that made the leaves shake on the trees. The dead boar beside him was by far the biggest living creature Nick had ever seen, but now even that was dwarfed by the approaching monster.

Nick looked for the closest place to hide. A dense bush grew a few yards away. There was no time to stand and run. Nick skittered on hands and knees into the bush, rolling the last yard into the shadows of its branches. He stopped, facing back toward the dead boar, just as the thing entered the forest clearing. It was a giant. No—*ogre* was a better word for this ugly thing. Nick's eyes closed involuntary the first time he saw the face.

The ogre stood over the dead boar and prodded it with one foot. He chuckled loudly, an evil sound that made the bones in Nick's chest vibrate like a tuning fork. The ogre reached into the branches of the tree and, taking hold of a rope, hoisted the spiked contraption. The boar slid free of the bloody spikes with a squishy noise that made Nick's stomach turn. The ogre pried open the metal jaws that held the boar's leg and busied himself resetting the trap. Nick marveled at the ingenious system of metal parts and ropes and pulleys that seized the prey, brought down the killing spikes, and sent the signal flag aloft in the trees. It was more cleverly constructed than anything Nick had seen in the world below.

From his hiding place just a few feet away, Nick got a long look at the gruesome being. He was so massive that a tall man like Finch wouldn't reach his knees. For the most part, he looked like a person enlarged to gargantuan size, but the proportions were somehow distorted. The arms hung too low, past the knees. The fingers were too long. They were bony and big at the knuckles, and swollen again at the tips, with nails that tapered off into pointy talons, gray and hard as shovels.

And that face. It was three parts human—but one part something else. The elongated snout with a twitching nose at the end; the fine, sharp, yellow teeth that jutted this way and that; the nasty colored skin, a splotchy marble of pink and gray; the long tangles of hair that might have been white except for the filth, hanging sloppily over his sloped shoulders . . . it all reminded Nick of some earthly animal. A rat?

But it was more than mere ugliness that struck fear deep into Nick's soul. It was the sneer on his face and the way he dressed. The ogre wore a vest and pants made from the skins of strange animals. It was a patchwork of tans, grays, and blacks, crudely stitched together, and there were mummified heads still in place among the pelts.

Hideous jewelry decorated the ogre. Around his throat was a necklace made of the skulls of his prey, with a chain threaded through the empty eye sockets. A set of keys hung on the chain as well. From one ear, an earring dangled; it was made from another skull, with the elongated jaws of some reptilian beast clamped onto the lobe in a mock death bite. The longer Nick looked, the more loathsome the ogre seemed.

The monster was nearly done with his chore. He covered the leg trap with armfuls of fallen leaves. Then he lifted the corpse as easily as Nick could lift a dead cat and stuffed it into a sack. He slung it merrily over his shoulder and walked off the way he had come.

Abruptly, the ogre stopped and turned back toward the clearing. His gaze dropped toward the undergrowth where Nick was hiding. Through the unkempt strands of hair that fell across his forehead, the ogre's eyes scanned the ground. They were terrible pink eyes with blood-red irises at the center. Nick kept perfectly still, except for the trembling hands he could not control. For a terrible moment, he thought the ogre was sniffing the air, and he remembered Jack's giant, smelling the blood. . . .

But then the ogre looked to the sky, shielding his face from the sun with one hand. All the while, his raw pink nose was twitching furiously. Something was puzzling the monster, but Nick could not tell what it was.

At last the ogre turned back toward the castle. His thumping footsteps died away like a receding drum, and then he was gone.

Nick flopped onto his back and filled his chest with a deep draft of air. His thoughts were a muddle, and the awful headache that the boar's tusk had given him was making it hard to think. He put his hands to his temples and grabbed fistfuls of his own hair. He shook his head back and forth, barely able to believe what he had just seen: an ogre, bigger than a house, close enough to touch.

This adventure had taken a malignant turn. Maybe it would be best to get back down the beanstalk as fast as he could.

Nick crawled out from under the bush. *Here are your choices,* he thought, standing up. *Climb down right now, as poor as you started. And then what? More begging, more stealing? Live in fear of meeting Finch and his gang again?*

"I'd rather get eaten alive by that ogre," he said aloud.

So that means you stay up here for now. And you either go to the giant's castle, or explore somewhere else. The castle, as the story goes, is where the treasure lies. It also must be the home of that awful ogre. But where else would you go? Toward that far-off mountain? That's a long way to walk—will the beanstalk still be here when you get back? And is the way filled with dangers like that boar, or worse?

The more he thought, the clearer the choice became. It was a simple plan, really. All he had to do was go to the castle, wait for the ogre to leave, steal the treasures within, and climb down the beanstalk a wealthy boy. If Jack could do that so many years ago, then Nick could do it today.

He was about to move on when a sound caught his ear. It was a familiar sound in the world Nick came from: the ringing of a cowbell. At first it seemed distant, but as it tolled every few seconds, each clang was closer than the one before. Nick would have hidden again, but he could not tell where the sound was coming from. At last it rang out loud and strong, directly behind a thick clump of the beanstalk vines. Whatever it was, it was out of sight behind that wall of green. Then the vines rustled, and they came alive like a mass of snakes and parted at the middle, rolling back in curls. In the space between were a man and a cow of ordinary size.

The forest fell silent. The black birds that flew and called ceaselessly overhead alighted on branches and cocked their heads to look down.

The man sat on a stool beside the cow, and the cow craned its neck out to munch on a leaf of the beanstalk plant. In the man's hand was a metal cup with a slender handle. He brought it to his lips and drank. It was a long, loud sip.

"My, that's good. Fresh and warm, as I like it." He turned to look at Nick with an impish expression. "You know, lad, to a hungry man, a good cow is worth more than all the gold in the world. Can't drink gold, now, can you? Come and have some. You look a little hungry yourself. It might even do that aching head of yours some good," the man said, tapping his temple with one finger.

Nick hesitated, watching the beanstalk vines that had parted like curtains. They were still disturbingly alive, waving about on either side.

"Don't fret about them, lad. You've got bigger worries up here, don't you." The man held out the cup. Nick took it with both hands and guzzled the milk. It was warm, almost steaming, creamy and sweet. Nick held the cup upside-down to let every last drop fall into his open mouth, then handed it back to the grinning man.

"Thank you," said Nick. "Guess I was thirsty." His stomach felt wonderfully warm and nourished. And not only that, but his throbbing headache had faded away.

Nick took a closer look at the man before him, who simply gazed back and smiled. There didn't seem to be anything unusual about the fellow at first glance. But the closer Nick looked, the odder he seemed. Was he young or old? It was hard to tell. He was bald on top and his face was clean-shaven, but the hair on the sides and back of his head hung past his shoulders and was braided into three long tails. The hair was silvery white—but no, when Nick looked closer, it seemed as if all the colors in the world flashed in those locks. The clothes the man wore had the same effect. The material looked like ordinary wool, but finer threads were woven in that reflected the colors of everything around them.

Nick had met a few foreigners in his short life, but he could not imagine from where this fellow had come. His complexion was coppery and smooth, his features sharply angled. And his eyes were too big, too bright, too green, too full of light.

Staring into those emerald eyes, Nick was embarrassed to realize that he'd been gaping for an uncomfortably long time. The man laughed heartily as he saw Nick blush.

"As long as your mouth is hanging open, have you

something to ask me? Come now, Nick, I can't stay for long." The stranger gestured with long, slim fingers toward an hourglass at his feet. Nick gave it a passing glance—and then looked again, because something was happening that jarred his senses: The sparkling sand inside the green-tinted glass was flowing *up* instead of down, from the bottom of the hourglass to the top.

That wasn't the only startling thing that just happened. The stranger had called Nick by his name. It was unnerving enough when both Finch and Jack had been able to guess his thoughts, but this was worse. Nick wondered if it truly was the first time they met, because there was something familiar about that face. It even seemed that he'd seen this cow—this *particular* cow—somewhere before.

Nick searched his mind and found the answer. He had only glanced at that painting in Jack's gallery briefly, yet he was sure this was the mysterious stranger that traded his magic beans for Jack's cow. But sixty years or more had passed since that day, and Nick's thoughts grew dizzy as he tried to reconcile the decades that had elapsed with the sight of the man and beast before him.

"Who are you, sir?" he asked at last.

"Ha!" roared the mysterious stranger. "That's a fine question, coming from one who is not even sure who *he* is! I won't answer that until the day you can do the same." He leaned back against the cow and folded his arms, apparently awaiting the next question.

"I know who you are, anyway," said Nick. "You're the fellow who swapped the beans for Jack's cow—the one that started all this. Why did you do it?"

The stranger just raised an eyebrow and waited some more, declining to respond.

"Well . . . what is this place, this island? Can you tell me that?" Nick asked.

"Hmmm. That I can tell, but how to say it in a way you can understand?" The stranger thought for a moment, scratching his chin with the tip of his little finger. "You've heard the tale of Noah and his ark, no doubt?"

"I have."

"Then consider this island in the clouds a kind of ark, for the creatures and treasures of myth and magic that, belonging on earth no more, were sent away."

"Sent away by whom? And why?"

The stranger waved off the question with one hand. "Too long an answer for too short a visit."

Nick glanced at the hourglass. Nearly half the sand had flown up, but he had so many more questions. "Tell me then, why did my beanstalk come to the same place as Jack's beanstalk, right near the castle? Was that just by chance?"

"Is it only happenstance when the robin returns in spring, and chooses the same tree to build its nest? Or when the master abandons the dog and the dog finds the master?"

Nick sighed. The stranger's cryptic answers were

maddening. He knew plenty, that was certain, but Nick doubted he could extract information of any value at all. Not even the fellow's name. *Well,* Nick thought, *I'll just give you a name: Greeneyes.* It was probably a name the stranger had been called before.

The green-eyed man leaned forward on his stool, gazing sharply. "Now, Nick, I have a question. Answer me true. Why have you come? What do you want here?"

Nick thought for a while. What did he want? Food in his belly every night. A place to sleep. A refuge from wicked men. Maybe up here, he could find the wealth he needed to afford these things.

"I want the giant's gold," he replied at last.

Greeneyes smiled. "And why not? Look at you, with your skin stretched tight over those bones. Can't blame you for wanting to escape your misery. But are you the only one here who seeks escape? Perhaps not, little thief."

Enough riddles, Nick thought angrily. "What do you mean?"

"I mean it is curious you chose to arrive at this moment—this dangerous moment. But don't worry about that—it need not affect you. Go to the castle, Nick. There are treasures in abundance! You'll know the room when you see it. The door is locked, but that is no use against a mouse like you. Although," Greeneyes said, with one eye narrowed and the other sparkling bright, "there will be other doors, won't there?

Other doors, other choices, other dangers . . ."

Nick's anger boiled up inside. "Why all these hints? Why the mysteries? Just tell me what you mean. What do you want from me?"

The plants on either side of the clearing rustled, and the vines crept back toward the center, like curtains closing on the act of a play. Nick stepped back, out of their way. The stranger lifted his hourglass, where the last of the sand was about to rise through the narrow center.

"Time's almost up," Greeneyes said, grinning at his joke. "Remember, lad, boys like you come up to make mischief—but the real trouble's what might come *down*."

His voice grew fainter as he talked, and the vines met and intertwined before the place he'd stood, surrounding and concealing Greeneyes and the cow. The last thing Nick saw was those glittering eyes before the swarming vines covered the man completely. All at once, the crows renewed their raucous chorus in the branches and sky overhead.

Greeneyes was gone, and it was hard to believe he had ever been there at all.

Nick's headache was cured, but his brain was spinning from the conversation. He wondered who Greeneyes was, how he got here, why he appeared, why he vanished. For that matter, why did he give Jack those beans so many years ago?

At least the stranger revealed one thing: There were

things of great value somewhere in the castle. If Nick could find them and get out alive, he could grow up as rich as Jack.

Nick took a step in the direction of the castle, but he stopped when he heard the voice shouting out from behind him, from such a distance he could barely be heard.

"Mind your step, Nick! Would you walk into the same trap as those who have gone before you?"

Nick looked at his feet. He was so flustered by the encounter that he'd forgotten the ogre's trap and nearly walked right through the spot where the boar was killed. The ground was still muddy with the blood of the beast. Nick stepped gingerly back from danger, unsure where the trigger lay. He turned back to look for Greeneyes, but the vines remained closed around that spot.

"Careful, Nick," he said to himself. "Let's not get ourselves killed."

Walking a wide circle around the trap, Nick headed for the castle. He found the path that the ogre took, where the undergrowth was trampled flat and branches twenty-five feet up on both sides had been snapped off. Nick followed that trail until it met a larger path. This was a wide swath that drove in a straight line through the forest. Everything here had been pulled up or hacked away. The stumps of the largest trees were chopped to within a foot of the ground. Some rocks had been tossed to the side; others were smashed to pieces, and their fragments were scattered all about. Deep wheel-worn grooves ran parallel down the center of the road.

Turning one way would take him back toward the beanstalk. Nick went the other way, toward the castle. He walked as quietly as possible. He kept his head turning always, looking to each side for boars or other unknown threats, and watching ahead in case the ogre came back down the path.

Soon the road emerged from the forest into a meadow of tall grass. Glimpsing beyond it, Nick got his first close look at the giant's castle.

It was a gloomy, foreboding place of awesome dimensions. To build it, the giant must have used an entire mountain's worth of stones. Or perhaps a mountain once stood on this spot and the giant simply tore it apart and reassembled it as this monstrosity.

An entire village could have fit inside its outer walls. Ten of Jack's houses, stacked like children's blocks, would not have reached as high. Unlike the straight lines and tidy angles of Jack's creation, this place sprawled recklessly, its walls bulging in places, meandering out and around and coming together as if by chance on the other side.

A tower erupted at one corner of the castle and a strange device was in motion at its apex. Radiating out and spinning slowly were three broad triangular sails, each stretched between a pair of wooden poles. Nick wondered what made them go. Then a stiff breeze arose, and he noticed that the sails spun faster. *It's the wind*, he realized.

Thin black smoke leaked out at the tower's peak. The whirling sails of the wind machine swept it away.

The castle was built high on a craggy ledge and hemmed by a hellish jumble of rocks, perhaps the debris from its ancient construction. To approach, Nick would have to take the dirt road that went past the main door, or climb across the mess of rocks to either side. He didn't like the looks of the shadowy places among those boulders, but at least they offered a place to hide if the ogre emerged.

Keeping low in the tall grass, Nick ran across the meadow and began to pick his way across the rocks. Crows had been plentiful enough in the forest, but they absolutely infested the castle grounds. As Nick drew closer to the castle, he saw what attracted them here. All around the castle were the gnawed bones of animals. Some were bleached under the sun. Others were fresh, and the crows cawed and sparred over the bits of flesh that still clung to them. Among the bones, Nick saw skulls of animals that looked totally unfamiliar to him, heads that sprouted exotic horns and antlers. The bones were strewn in such a random manner that Nick assumed they were merely tossed over the wall when the ogre finished his meal. A foul stench of rot filled the air, and he pulled the neckline of his shirt over his nose to ward it off.

Nick came under the shadows of the walls at one side of the front door. Below the door was a gap that he could easily squeeze through.

A few of the crows nearby suddenly took flight. Nick hunched low, alert to danger. Over the screech of the birds, he heard a growing, rhythmic creaking. It reminded him of the sound of the wagon that he robbed in the forest, but its volume was far greater.

He didn't see anything coming along the road he'd followed. But that same path disappeared around the far side of the castle. Something on wheels was approaching from that direction, and any moment now it would come into view.

Nearby, two tall slabs of discarded stone leaned against each other, with a deep crevice between them. Nick darted into it.

He instantly regretted this choice of hiding places. A gluey spider web, its gray threads as thick as rope, spanned the width of the crevice just inside the opening. Stuck all over the web, instead of flies, were the mummified bodies of crows. The web blocked the way into the safe recesses of the crevice, so Nick was left with precious little room to conceal himself from the approaching danger. He looked behind the web. A yawning funnel of spun silk vanished into the darkness. As his eyes began to adapt to the gloom, Nick thought he could make out a pair of glinting eyes deep inside.

There was no time to find another place to hide. A second ogre was coming into view on the road, pulling a noisy cart behind him. Nick flattened himself against the rock, barely out of the daylight, doing his best to remain out of sight. He hoped his black garments would once again help him merge into the shadows.

This ogre was larger and more brutish than the one Nick encountered in the forest, distinct in appearance but no less horrible. He was almost as wide as he was tall, with a thick chest, a fat belly, and colossal muscles on his arms and legs. His skin was gray, hairless, and covered with warty lumps. His eyes were bulging and enormous, his slobbering mouth went nearly ear to ear, and his nose was nothing more than a long pair of runny holes. If the first ogre seemed to have the essence of rat in his recipe, this one had a dash of toad. But then again, no toad Nick had ever seen had a mouth filled with awful yellow teeth.

Like the first ogre, this one wore animal hides. But his clothes were more bedraggled, just a tattered vest and pants that were ripped to shreds below the knees. No hideous jewelry decorated this monster.

The toad-ogre had over his shoulders a harness, which he used to pull a great two-wheeled cart behind him. Nick recognized what was being hauled: It was a gigantic heap of the vines that resembled the beanstalk.

The ogre shrugged off the harness and let the front of the cart tilt to rest on the ground. He arched his back and stretched his arms. Then, like the ogre in the forest had done, he looked at the ground with a puzzled expression. Nick dared to stick his head out another inch to see what the monster was looking at. He appeared to be staring at the shadow of the cart.

Then, again like the first ogre, this one stared at the sun. He scratched his head. Nick could not understand what was confusing the ogres. Something about the shadows?

Nick reminded himself to keep an eye on the web behind him. He turned around and nearly cried out when he saw the abhorrent creature that had crept out of the dark funnel and mounted the opposite side of the web.

It had the hairy jointed legs of a spider. But where a spider's body should have been was the head of a human being. The skin was dry and shriveled like a raisin, with black and purple veins pulsing just underneath. Behind the head was a mushy sack of flesh that ended in a point, with a strand of thread oozing from the tip.

The head tilted to one side, and the creature looked at Nick with curious red-rimmed eyes. Then, to Nick's horror, it smiled at him. There were no teeth in that mouth, just a tiny black tongue and a pair of fangs that pinched and opened like tongs. Nick saw a trembling drop of venom at the tip of one fang. The spider-head put a leg between the strands of the web and reached for him. The crusty leg ended in a cluster of soft, wiggling human fingers.

Nick reached into his pocket for the knife. He unfolded the blade and held the point out toward the foul thing. "Get away from me," he said quietly but sharply, with his teeth clamped together.

The spider-head seemed to understand the threat. Its smile curved downward into a frown. It opened and closed its mouth as if it was trying to speak, but it could only mewl like a kitten. Then it crawled down the web and shuffled backward into the darkness, staring at him with longing eyes.

Nick watched it go. The ogres were fearsome, but this creature inspired a mixture of loathing and pity. He wondered what hideous forces could have conspired to create such an abomination.

A commotion drew Nick's attention, and he looked back toward the ogre. The monster was banging with powerful fists on the castle door, and hollering in a thunderous voice. Nick could almost understand what the ogre was saying—even pick out some fragments of words here and there—but most of it was gibberish.

The castle door swung open, and the rat-ogre was there. He took one look at the harvest in the cart and began to scream. But this time Nick understood every word.

"Idiot! Is this where you've been all day? I told you a hundred times," the rat-ogre roared, now emphasizing every word by slapping the top of the toad-ogre's head, "We! Don't! Need! Any! More!"

The rat-ogre chased the other inside, kicking him in the rear, still screaming. "Basher the fool! Basher the half-wit!" The door slammed shut behind them. The screaming died away as they went into the depths of the castle.

Despite the danger, Nick found himself a little

amused by the scene he'd witnessed. He'd also learned a great deal. The evil-tempered rat-ogre was the clever one, probably the one that built the trap in the forest. The rat-ogre was able to talk, while "Basher" could make only crude attempts at speech. And the rat-ogre was clearly in charge, even though the other was larger and stronger.

But where did these behemoths come from? Were they invaders from somewhere else on the vast cloud island, who seized control of the castle when its owner departed?

An alarm sounded in Nick's brain, and he remembered to check on the spider-head just in time. He didn't see the creature when he turned around, but the web was quivering. He looked up and saw it dropping from above, suspended from its thread, and reaching for him with both forelegs. Nick slashed with his knife and sliced the fingers off the end of one leg. A black-red fluid spattered the rocks below. The spider-head let loose a high-pitched squeal that stung Nick's ears. He didn't wait for a counterattack. He jumped out of the crevice and flew to the front door. Without hesitating, he slid underneath and entered the giant's castle.

On the other side of the door, Nick found himself in a gigantic hall, thankfully alone. It didn't seem possible to build anything this big, with a ceiling so high and walls so distant from each other. It was constructed with the same distorted architecture as the outer walls. The walls heaved and curved in random fashion. Straight lines were scarce to be seen. A handful of twisted columns, positioned without symmetry, rose to support the domed roof. It felt more like standing in a cavern than a hall.

The ceiling was decaying. Chunks had fallen out, and the sun streamed through those gaping holes, thrusting swords of light through the dusty air. The ever-present crows had found their way through the gaps, and they glided, screeching, in the vastness overhead.

There were still remnants of beauty in the hall, but decades of neglect and abuse left them utterly ruined. Tapestries on the walls were mostly shredded, and the parts that were still intact were so dirty that their designs were obscured. There had been furniture, but now it lay in splinters. There had been great marble sculptures, but only the shattered pieces remained.

Nick was so shaken by the encounter with the spider-head, he'd forgotten to breathe. He inhaled deeply. Then he clapped a hand over his mouth to keep himself from spitting up. The time he spent getting accustomed to the smell while hiding outside did not prepare him for the putrid air inside the castle. He tried breathing through his mouth, but that was worse—he could actually *taste* the foul odor.

On the opposite side of the hall, an archway led into the kitchen. Nick recognized the scene at once, from the painting of the giant in Jack's gallery that had given him such a fright. The kitchen table with tree trunks for legs was still there, and a few of the familiar chairs stood around it. These were among the handful of pieces of furniture that were still intact.

A gaping fireplace occupied the far wall of the kitchen. A fire was blazing there, its flames leaping ten feet high. The dead boar, its hide removed, was mounted on a skewer above the flames.

The skewer was being turned, but not by hand. A thick rope came through one of the holes in the ceiling. It was threaded through an iron ring that stuck out from the stone wall above the fireplace, and knotted to the handle that turned the skewer. The rope rose and fell, pulled taut and relaxed; and as it did so, the boar spun over the fire. Nick wondered what was making the rope move, and then remembered the turning sails of the wind machine on the castle tower.

On each side of the hall, smaller arches led to hallways into the rest of the castle's interior. Nick heard bellowing and heavy footsteps coming from one of those passages; the sound echoed back and forth across the cavernous hall. The ogres were approaching.

Hiding places were plentiful in the rubble on the floor. Nick crept into a smashed piece of pottery that hid him from view. He peeked through a crack and spied on the ogres as they came into the room. Basher was blathering incoherently, but the rat-ogre seemed to understand him well enough.

"Can't you even wait until it's cooked? Fine, then," the

rat-ogre said. Holding the end of the skewer, he pulled the boar from the fire and tossed it onto the table. "Eat it raw."

Basher sat and tore into the beast with ravenous glee.

"I'll get my own dinner. Another flag's up, anyway. Besides, I have to make certain nothing is blocking the road after that windstorm." The rat-ogre took his blood-stained sack and headed across the hall to the door. He turned before leaving, and snarled back, "And don't sleep the time away while I'm gone! You know what needs to be done around here!" The rat-ogre left without closing the door.

Nick was glad to see one of the ogres leave. Now if Basher would go, he could explore the castle and seek out its treasures.

From the table in the kitchen came the loud sounds of slurping, chewing and crunching. Nick watched Basher licking his fingers, one by one. Red juice was rolling down the ogre's face like a mountain stream. He had consumed the boar with amazing speed. What was on the table was no longer a recognizable animal; it was just a pile of gnawed and broken bones. Basher reached one arm across the table and swept the whole mess onto the floor. Then he folded his arms and rested his head upon them. Before a minute passed, he was snoring loudly.

Nick came slowly out of hiding. This was his chance to explore—until Basher woke up or the other one returned to the castle, whichever came first.

There were two hallways to choose from, leading to the wings of the castle. Nick let his nose decide. While the general stench in the castle was hard to take, the stink that flowed from the hall on the right seemed unbearable. He chose the one to his left.

It was time to steal a fortune of his own.

CHAPTER 12

Jack and his men approached the crest of the hill. The horses struggled to pull the wagon up the steep grade, even though only Jack was riding now. Henry walked in front, guiding the pair of horses, and Roland and Bill walked beside the wagon. The young men were ready for combat. They wore leather armor, with swords at their sides and bows slung across their backs. Spears and other weapons were heaped in the back of the wagon.

From behind the hill, they saw only the upper reaches of the beanstalk. When they came to the top, the entire growth would come into view, less than a half mile away. As that moment approached, the excitement grew among Jack's men. They glanced at one another, smiling nervously. And they looked back at their master riding in the wagon. But Jack did not meet their gaze. He kept his eyes on the great dark cloud that seemed ready to smother the Earth like a pillow over its face.

A hundred feet shy of the top, Jack told Henry to stop

the wagon. Roland went to help the old man, but Jack waved him off. He clambered down, then signaled for his men to follow him up. When the old man was almost to the ridge, he went to his hands and knees and crawled the final yards. His men did likewise. Four across, they came to the edge on their bellies and, for the first time, saw the awesome beanstalk in its entirety, from its deeply driven roots to the point where it practically vanished high above.

Jack looked at his men. They were thrilled, amazed, and a bit frightened. Natural reactions, Jack supposed. For him this was a distant memory revisited. But for these three, it was a strange and magical intrusion into their ordinary lives. Jack had never revealed to even his most trusted servants the absolute truth of his story of the beanstalk and the giant. Over the years, they watched him paint the scenes in finer detail than any imagination could conceive. They saw the long-dead hen and the staggering cache of golden eggs in his vault. But Jack knew that, despite all that evidence, his servants were still sure it was all nothing more than a fabrication. Like the rest of the folk in this land, they came to regard him as a harmless eccentric who enjoyed spinning a tall tale. And who could blame them for doubting?

But now the beanstalk vaulted into the heavens before their eyes, more massive than any living thing they'd seen, and a surreal dark cloud straddled the land. Jack could imagine what his men were thinking. Here was proof of the existence of otherworldly things. And if the beanstalk was real, then it was all real: the man-eating giant, the castle in the clouds, the fantastic treasures.

Their eyes sparkled with tears of wonder. Seeing the look on one another's faces, all four men laughed softly.

"It actually happened," said Roland, the first to speak. "And you really climbed that thing, all the way up, didn't you?"

"All the way," replied Jack with a grin, wiping his eye with his sleeve.

"And the giant, and the giant's wife?" asked Bill. "Just like you painted them?"

"Just like that."

"It can't be," said Henry.

Roland closed his eyes and opened them again. He seemed surprised that the beanstalk was still there.

"Look there," said Bill, pointing down. There was a group of men around the foot of the beanstalk. Some sat smoking pipes. Others rested in the shade of a little ramshackle farmhouse. They seemed to be waiting.

"Henry, are those your friends from the forest?" asked Jack.

"I . . . I can't tell from here," said Henry in a tight voice. "They might be." He clearly didn't like the possibility of encountering those thugs again. The four of them had taken the forest road on the way to the beanstalk, and when they passed the spot where the assault took place, Henry couldn't stop his limbs from shaking.

"Does anyone see the boy?" asked Jack. None of them did. Jack thought for a while, tugging at his silver beard.

"Henry, I need to ask a favor of you," said Jack.

"Yes, Master Jack."

"I'd like you to get a closer look at those men. See if it isn't the same gang that set upon you in the forest. And tell me if that skinny boy is with them, perhaps dressed all in black. If you approach from that direction, you should be able to get close without being seen." Jack indicated a place farther south along the ridge. There a thicket extended from the edge of the farmland, quite close to the beanstalk, and grew up the hillside.

Roland saw Henry begin to tremble as Jack issued his instructions. "Master Jack, let me go instead. Henry's had one run-in with that crew; he doesn't need another."

"That's good of you, Roland. But Henry, I think you should be the one. Only you can recognize the band of thieves for certain. Also I want a runner, not a fighter, and I know you are swift of foot. If you're in danger, promise me you'll just run back here as fast as you can."

"I will," said Henry. Roland frowned, but he knew better than to argue.

Henry ran a hand across his forehead and through his hair, and sighed deeply. "Well, the sooner gone, the sooner back." He started off, moving quickly but carefully, staying behind the crest of the ridge where he could not be seen by the men in the valley below.

Jack watched him and considered the other reason he

wanted Henry to go. *Better to face your fears sooner than later, Henry. Trust me on that.*

Henry moved south along the ridge until he reached the area above the thicket. Trees grew more than halfway up the slope, so he would only be out in the open for a short time before reaching cover. He moved as fast as he could across the exposed ground, watching for loose rocks under his feet and glancing over at the gang at the base of the beanstalk. No one turned and pointed in his direction or gave any other indication that he was seen.

Ann would have loved to see this, he thought as he glanced up at the towering plant. She certainly put up a fuss when Jack said she could not come. But Jack must have known there would be danger. And with this band of villains about, it was no place for a young girl.

As Henry drew closer to the beanstalk's trunk, darting from tree to tree, he noticed a change in the woods around him. Everywhere else in the land, leaves still clung to the trees and bushes. But near the beanstalk, the branches were bare except for a few leaves that stubbornly hung on, brown and dry. The grasses were dead and crisp weeks before their time. The earth itself was as arid as a desert. He kicked up a thin cloud of dust with every step.

Henry heard a strange mix of noises in the ground beneath him, one like a hiss, another like rolling subterranean thunder. It wasn't hard to guess the cause of these strange effects: The milky green roots of the beanstalk were everywhere.

Moving stealthily forward, Henry drew within a stone's throw of the beanstalk. He crawled on his belly under a dying evergreen shrub that shed its needles at the slightest touch.

A few feet to Henry's right, the earth heaved and split open. A massive green thing, round and muscular as a snake, humped up through the opening. His heart was pounding so wildly he could hear it thumping inside his chest. Then the monstrous thing vanished again deep into the soil. It was one of the mighty roots of the beanstalk, perhaps shifting itself to probe deeper for more water. It reminded Henry of a whale he once watched coming to the surface of the ocean and diving again into the foamy gray depths. *Its thirst must be incredible*, Henry thought, *to sustain such growth. No wonder it's sucking the earth dry, even stealing life from the vegetation around it.*

"Remember what you're here for, Henry," he muttered to himself. He turned his attention to the men gathered around the beanstalk. His teeth ground together as he recognized the murderous crew that attacked him in the forest and stole the trunk of books. *As if any of them could read,* he thought. Henry's anger grew as he recognized the vilest one, tall and toothless. That was a face he could never forget.

Henry was surprised to discover that his fear had

almost vanished. He found himself enjoying the excitement of his mission. Spying on this evil collection of thugs was a small but satisfying measure of revenge.

He studied them for a while to see if a small boy dressed in black might be among them.

CHAPTER 13

The hallway was long and dark, narrow for ogres but wide as a river to Nick. It was dirty, but not as cluttered as the kitchen or the great hall. Nick was on edge as he ran down it, because there was nowhere to hide. He knew the rat-ogre was off on some errand, and he could hear Basher's snores even here. But could he be sure those were the only gigantic beings in the castle?

Cobwebs were everywhere, some of normal size and some spun from the same thick cord as the web of the ghastly spider-head Nick had met outside the castle. He saw none of those nightmarish creatures, only the filthy gray tunnels where they might have been sleeping. In the dark recesses of one web, high overhead where the wall met the ceiling, Nick thought he saw a furtive movement and a pair of glowing eyes that blinked once and went dark. He did not linger there. He went on, moving faster, feeling as vulnerable as a mouse creeping through the lair of a cat.

Halfway through the hall, Nick came to a pair of doors, one on either side. The door on the right was a simple wooden one. It had a small square opening at what would have been eye level for an ogre, but was far too high for Nick to peer through. The door was secured with a padlock. Nick recalled the set of keys that dangled from the chain around the rat-ogre's neck.

The door on the left was another matter. It too was made of wood, but it was reinforced with wide and heavy bands of iron. It had not one but three separate locks on it, all sturdier than the one that protected the other doorway.

That means there's something inside worth protecting, he thought.

He looked at the base of the door. There was only a slender opening at his feet, too narrow for him to squeeze through. But near the hinged side of the door, there was a depression in the stone floor. It would be a tight fit, but he thought he could make it.

Nick knew the trick would be getting his head and shoulders through first. If those could pass, the rest of him would follow. He lay on his back and began to wiggle through. The fit was so tight he had to turn his face to one side to avoid bumping his nose. Still, the wood scraped roughly over his cheek. His head emerged on the other side and his shoulders came next. He pulled his hands through and, pushing against the door, squirmed through to his waist. Then he sat up, facing the door, and slid his legs out from underneath.

When he stood and turned to face the room, he was looking at more treasure than he had dared to dream for.

This was the smallest room he'd seen so far, but it was packed with objects of incredible value, ransoms for a thousand kings. There were a dozen iron bowls, as wide across as Nick's outstretched arms and so deep their sides came up to his waist. Each was filled with eggs of gold, like the ones Nick tried to steal from Jack's gallery. The giant must have been hoarding them for years when the hen was his.

There was a chest filled with cut and polished gems, glittering white, green, red, and blue. The box was so full its lid could no longer close. Hundreds of the fat stones had simply rolled off the pile and lay scattered on the floor.

There were sacks of every size piled against one wall. A couple had fallen and burst open, spilling out gold and silver coins as wide as dinner plates.

Shelves soared along the other walls, and they were lined with artifacts that looked like the works of a lost civilization. Nick saw priceless statuettes, cast in gold and other precious metals, studded with diamonds and rubies and emeralds. Some were in the shape of animals, some human, and some a mad mix, both human and beast.

There were also giant weapons on those shelves: daggers, swords, spears, and axes, all encrusted with jewels.

And a hundred other objects, from crowns to necklaces to urns to shields.

In that room there must have been more wealth than was held in the vaults of all the nobles in the world below. It was too much to comprehend. Nick's legs wobbled, and he had to sit on the ground to avoid falling.

"Use your head, Nick," he said. "You found it. Now you have to get away with it."

He turned his mind to the problem. He would take it one trip at a time. Grab as many valuables as he could safely carry—and fit under the door—and bring them to the top of the beanstalk. Then, if he got his nerve up, return again for a second trip, and perhaps even a third if things went smoothly. After all, it shouldn't be hard to slip in and out of the castle unseen. The ogres didn't know he was here. And the more trips he made, the richer he would be.

Nick found a sack of useful size, filled with gold coins. It would have fit easily into one of the ogre's pockets, but for him, it was perfect to sling over his back. He emptied all of the coins out but one. Then he refilled it with gems of every color, a few gold eggs, and a small statue that bristled with jewels. He cinched the top and hefted it. It was too heavy, so he dug out some of the goods and tossed them on the floor. When he tried once more, he could swing it over his back easily.

Nick turned to take another look around the room to see if he was missing anything of extraordinary value.

There was one object he hadn't noticed before. Something the size of a man, tucked away in the darkest corner, behind a chest, as if to keep it out of sight. It was covered with a piece of cloth—the only thing in the room concealed in that fashion.

Curious, Nick put the sack down and walked over. He held onto one corner of the cloth and stepped back. The cloth slid over the top of the object and whispered to the ground.

It was a figurine—a figurine to the giants, anyway; to Nick it was a statue a foot taller than himself. It was solid gold, and molded in the exact likeness of the rat-ogre. The ogre appeared to be in deep thought. With one hand, he cradled his chin between thumb and forefinger. With the long finger of the other hand, he pointed to his temple. Whatever he was thinking, they were not good thoughts. There was no mistaking the pure malevolence in that expression, in the narrow eyes and leering grin.

Nick stepped closer. The figure was so lifelike, in every detail, in every strand of hair and blemish of skin. He reached out to touch it. When his hands got close, he could sense a coldness emanating, as if it were carved from ice.

Nick touched it with one finger. It was cold, but not painfully so. He put both hands to the chest of the figurine. And he felt something begin to happen. It began to grow warmer; in seconds it was hot. Nick tried to pull away, but he could not. In fact his hands seemed to be drawn into the figurine, and the gold went soft and oozed between his fingers.

A jolt went through Nick's body, making his head snap back and his eyes roll up in their sockets. He forced his head back down and made his eyes focus on the figurine. The shape of the entire object was changing. The gold rippled and swirled, as if it suddenly turned to liquid.

The ogre melted away into a featureless mass, and then a new face and figure resolved themselves before Nick's eyes, and this one was even more familiar. It was Finch, fierce and grim. One blob of gold emerged from the shoulder and became an arm, and its hand went to the top of Nick's head and pushed it back to expose his throat. The other arm went up high, muscles straining, and out of the fist grew Finch's jagged knife, eager to slash. But Nick wasn't just seeing the image of the master thief, he was *feeling* the *essence* of the evil man, in flash after flash of awful insight, and he felt the endless greed and the bottomless appetite for violence, and he knew the burning eye and the bared tooth and the bloody blade, and Nick was sickened as he felt the joy of the kill, and the stony heart that knew no remorse. He saw the barely contained monster behind Finch's handsome exterior, the one he'd only sensed before when he looked through that false smile. And as soon as Nick thought about that smile it appeared on the face of the figurine, and Finch's eyes fixed upon his, radiating menace.

With a moan of agony, Nick tried to wrench his hands free, desperate to escape the awful empathy it was imposing on him, but they only sank deeper into the heart of the figurine. Then the metal glowed and went hotter still, and the shape began to change again. Finch's features blurred like wax over flame, and a new face emerged.

It was Old Man Jack, and as the likeness resolved itself, a new feeling rushed into Nick's consciousness. It was sadness, only sadness, as deep and dark and endless as the ocean on a moonless night. Regret was a chain that wrapped around his throat and his arms and his legs and dragged him down, and for a lifetime he had fought and kicked and swam to keep his head above the waves. But the tugging burden was relentless, and down he would go, and the ocean was miles and miles deep, and he sank and sank, expecting to find the bottom, but always there were new depths of darkness and despair. Just when Nick thought his own heart would break from this glimpse inside the old man's everlasting guilt, the figurine spared him, and it began to change for the last time, and when it was done, the metal cooled and repelled Nick's hands, pushing them up and off of the surface, and the gold was like ice once more.

Nick backed away, weak and shaken by the powerful currents of raw emotion that had surged through his mind. And now he was seeing his own image in the figurine. Nick the boy thief was rendered in gold, in a skulking posture, a sack bulging with stolen goods flung across one shoulder. The expression was fearful and full of shame. It sickened him to look upon it.

Nick picked up the fallen cloth. He couldn't stand to look at his likeness for another moment. Besides, he did not want to leave evidence that he had been here. There was nothing he could do but conceal it and hope it was left undisturbed until he was long gone, beyond pursuit in the world below. Holding the cloth by one side, he snapped it into the air and it floated gently over his golden twin. *That's better*, he thought.

Before him, the rat-ogre must have been the last to touch the figurine, for that was the form it was in when Nick found it. The ogre must not have liked what the object had shown him either, and so he tucked it out of sight. How disturbing, to have something in common with that monster.

Nick felt dizzy, thinking about the visions he'd witnessed and what they might mean. He shook his head to clear his mind. *Don't think about it. Just do what you came to do and forget what you've seen.* He backed away from the figurine and returned to his collected treasure.

He dragged the sack over to the entrance. Then he lay on his back once more and slid his head under the door to make certain the hallway was empty.

Nick looked both ways and saw nothing. He heard the reassuring snores of the sleeping Basher from the faraway kitchen. Then he heard a new sound: the mournful cries of a woman.

He knew instantly that it was the voice of a giant. It was something he'd noticed when listening to the two ogres: the way he could feel the voice with his bones as well as hear it with his ears.

The heartbreaking sound was coming from behind the door on the other side of the hallway. The door with the little square opening in it, like a prison cell.

Nick frowned. Were there giants around every corner? He'd expected the castle to be empty after all these years.

Then a picture of a face popped into Nick's mind. It was the giantess from Jack's gallery. He remembered the long, bony features, the baggy gray eyes, the lump of a nose, the dark hair pulled back tight. It was a homely face for sure, but not an unpleasant one.

Most of all, Nick remembered the swollen belly that she cradled with one hand.

This voice—could it really be her, alive after all this time? *Who else could it be?*

And why was she crying—because she was a prisoner in that room?

That's none of your business, Nick told himself. *Don't make it your business.*

She was moaning, sobbing, muttering words. It sounded so lonely, so desperate, so profoundly sad. Something terribly wrong had happened to that woman. Nick lay on the floor, numbed by indecision.

In his hand, he held a sack filled with treasure, enough to make him wealthier than all but a few in the land he came from.

But beyond that other door was someone who sounded like she needed help. And if it turned out to be the giant's wife, what had she ever done to deserve misfortune? Nick knew the story; the giantess seemed like a decent sort. Maybe he could just poke his head under the prison door and take a peek.

Do that and you risk everything—the treasure and your life.

But if he just walked away without learning the reason for those cries, Nick knew he would carry the burden of not knowing forever.

Nick let go of the treasure. He crawled out from under the door and stood in the hallway.

The sack is right there for when you come back to it, he thought.

If you get back to it.

Nick's head whirled to the right as he heard another sound down the hallway. At the place where the corridor curved, he saw—or imagined he saw—a dark shape that ducked out of sight. He was jittery from his experience with the figurine, and he knew a nervous mind could trick itself, imagining the sounds and sights of danger where neither existed. It may have been nothing. Or it may have been the scrape of a foot on stone, and a glimpse of something on the prowl.

Nick took his knife from his pocket and unfolded the blade. He stood with his lower lip clamped between his teeth, staring at that spot in the corridor, waiting to see if something would poke its head around to stare back. He imagined himself playing a waiting game with whatever was around the corner, a test of wills to see who would lose patience and make the next move first. Perhaps one of the spider-heads would come scrabbling toward him. Or Greeneyes was on his trail, back to baffle him some more. A long time passed, but Nick saw nothing and heard only the woeful cries that continued behind the prison door. He relaxed a little, assured that the threat had only been in his mind. After a final glance down the corridor, he walked to the prison door and got on his belly to slide under.

What was it that Greeneyes had said? "*. . . there will be other doors, won't there? Other doors, other choices, other dangers . . .*"

He took a deep breath, then stuck his head under the door. It was an easier fit than the treasure room. Nick could hear the cries better but still could not see who was making them. He slid all the way through and sat on his haunches, scanning the room.

This place was even larger than the great hall, longer but narrower. There were windows here once, but stones blocked those openings now, perhaps to keep a prisoner from escaping. There were holes in the ceiling here as in the great hall, and the sunlight that streamed through provided the only illumination.

In the center of the room, just ahead of where Nick was standing, were two heaps of those beanstalk plants. In one stack, the vines were whole. The other, larger pile consisted of the shredded remains of vines. Either pile would have made a good-size hill in the world below.

The cries were coming from behind one of the mounds. Nick could see a huge bare foot poking out. Its owner was sitting or lying on the other side. He took two steps sideways, trying to get a better look without revealing himself entirely.

Beyond the piles, Nick saw a strange contraption that occupied the length of the far wall. It looked like the work of the same inventor who devised the deadly trap in the forest and the wind machine on the castle roof. With its long series of wheels arranged around a single shaft that passed down the middle like a spine, and the spindly legs that supported them all, it looked like a strange mechanical centipede.

A heavy rope hung through a hole in the ceiling, just as in the kitchen. It dangled above the machinery and bobbed up and down, disengaged, driven by the same relentlessly turning wind machine that powered the device in the kitchen. Having seen the way the rope in the kitchen made the boar turn over the fire,

Nick reasoned that when this one was attached, it would turn the shaft that ran the length of the machine, causing the iron wheels to spin.

But why? He could not begin to guess the purpose of all that machinery. Nick was so fascinated by it, he didn't notice that the mournful cries had ceased.

"Jack—is it really you?"

A massive head was leaning out from behind the pile of plants, looking directly at him. It was unmistakable: This was the giantess from Jack's painting. But she was older now. There was white in her hair. It was not combed neatly back anymore; it framed her face wildly. She was far thinner than Jack had drawn her; her wrinkled skin sagged everywhere, ending in loose folds that dangled under her chin. The eyes were the same steely gray, but a haze covered one eye. Her cheeks were damp with tears.

The giantess squinted hard as she looked at Nick. At first she seemed surprised, curious, even happy to see him. Then a suspicious look came across her face.

"No. Not Jack. Then who might you be, little boy?"

Nick spun around, meaning to duck under the door again.

"Stop!" she yelled with a ferocity that froze Nick in his tracks. "I'll call my sons if you take another step! If they know you're here, you won't get out alive."

Nick knew she was right. In that long hallway, with

nowhere to hide, the ogres—*her sons,* she'd said!—would run him down with a few great strides. He stood there on legs that felt like they had turned to jelly.

"Come here and sit." The giantess patted the ground beside her. "Now we will talk."

⊛ CHAPTER 14 ⊛

Nick had no choice but to do what the giantess said. She didn't seem murderous, like her sons. In fact she gave him an encouraging smile. She looked like a lonely soul who was glad to have some company. The best course of action, he decided, would be to win her confidence and wait for his chance to escape. Nick chose a spot just out of her reach and sat.

The giantess had been leaning on her elbow. She sat and crossed her legs, and her ancient bones creaked like a tall ship's timbers. "You came from down there, didn't you? From the land of little people."

"Yes, ma'am," said Nick.

"Did a strange vine bring you—a beanstalk?"

Nick nodded. "How did you know?"

The giantess raised her hand, dipping into one of the shafts of sunlight that entered through the broken ceiling. She looked at the shadow of her hand on the floor.

"I should have guessed sooner—when the shadows stopped dancing."

Nick understood at once the strange behavior of the ogres—why they had stared at the ground and looked to the sun, apparently confused. This was a cloud they lived on, not the solid and stable earth, where the sun and the stars navigated fixed and predictable courses. In this unearthly land, the sun was a nomad, its position forever changing as the cloud drifted and spun before the wind. How strange and beautiful it must be, thought Nick, to sit outside at night and watch the stars swirling around overhead.

On the cloud island, the sun wandered and the shadows danced—until the beanstalk rose out of the ground and summoned the island, seizing it and mooring it to one place.

"But why are you here, little man? Have you come to steal our precious things?"

"No, ma'am," Nick lied.

"Humph. That's what Jack said."

Judging from the tone of her voice, Nick thought it would be best not to mention his connection to Jack. He watched the giantess use one hand to rub the other, trying to soothe some ache, and noticed how damaged her hands seemed to be. The skin was cracked and dry, the joints badly swollen.

"Tell me your name, boy, and I'll tell you mine."

"My name is Nick."

"Mine is Gullinda."

A fat crow swooped over Gullinda's head. With alarming speed, she snatched the bird from the air. She popped it into her mouth, crunched it between her teeth, and swallowed it with a grimace.

Gullinda looked down at Nick. His hands were over his mouth and his eyes were bulging.

"Sorry. Woeful manners," she apologized. "I haven't had much in the way of food lately. But don't fear. I have no appetite for little people." A little black feather flew out of her mouth as she spoke. Nick watched it flutter down and land at his feet.

He took his hand off his mouth to ask a question. "Are . . . are you a prisoner here?"

The giantess nodded. "A prisoner and a slave, I am afraid."

"But who imprisoned you here? Not your own sons?"

Gullinda put her hands to her face, and nodded from behind them. Nick waited until, sniffling, she brought her hands down again.

"How . . . how long have they kept you here?"

"How long? I have lost track of the years. Thirty or more."

Nick almost fell over. Thirty years locked in that room. It was unthinkable. He stared around the room, at the thick stone walls and the heavy door. "Why would they do this? I have to help you out of here!"

Gullinda shook her head. "It is easy for you to slip in

and out, tiny one, but there is no escape for me. I have searched all these years for a way. What would you do— tear the stones from the wall? Break down that door? My son wears the key around his neck. And not the stupid one you hear snoring in the kitchen—my wicked, wily son. Would you dare to steal it from him?"

Nick did not try to answer. A painful silence followed.

He wondered how old Gullinda was. It was obvious that this race of giants lived far longer than people. The fact that she was still alive after all this time was evidence enough of that. Nick noticed that Gullinda seemed to be bigger—taller, anyway—than either of her sons. If the two were born shortly after Jack's adventure, that made them nearly sixty. But perhaps by ogre standards they were still young—hardly beyond boyhood.

Basher's snores were still audible in this room, but barely. He glanced nervously at the door.

Gullinda sensed his concern. "Ah, you needn't worry about Basher. If his belly is full, the lazy fool would sleep forever."

Nick gave her a weak smile. "What's the name of the rat—I mean, the other one?"

Gullinda's eyes narrowed. "That one calls himself Gnasher. Such clever names my boys chose for themselves: Gnasher and Basher. And where is that evil one now?"

"He said he was going to check the traps—and something about clearing the road." Nick blushed with guilt.

It was obvious he'd spied on the ogres. And why else would he spy except to steal?

"Then he will be gone for a long while. Now, little one, let us use this time wisely. You need to hear my tale. And when you have, you'll understand why you must go back to your world as fast as you can."

Nick scooted over, close to her side. "Go on," he said. "Tell me your story. And I will keep thinking about how to help you escape."

"My fate is sealed, young Nick. It is the fate of your world that you must concern yourself with now. And this is why." Gullinda looked over at the strange machinery. She plucked a piece of the plant from the pile and rolled it between her fingers. Then she closed her eyes and breathed deeply. When she opened them again, she wasn't looking at Nick anymore. She was looking through him and beyond him, thinking about things that happened long before.

"I had a husband once. A cruel and angry one. His name was Ramos."

Nick remembered the paintings of that awful giant in Jack's gallery. So, Ramos was his name.

"But one day Ramos troubled me no more. It had something to do with a boy like you—a boy named Jack, who came to our door one day while Ramos was gone. I fed him from our table, and he told me about his sorry life, and his land of little folk like yourself. How good it felt to have someone to talk to."

Gullinda waved her hand at the air. "Never mind—there is no time for that part of the tale now. All you must know is that Jack returned my kindness by stealing my husband's treasures while he slept. Three times Jack stole—until Ramos caught him at it. He thought I· was helping the boy. He threw me out of the way and kicked a chair in his rage, smashing his foot. And he swore he would kill me. Then he hobbled after the boy on his broken foot.

"I followed them in secret. I saw Jack climb down that strange beanstalk. And I watched my husband follow, off the misty edge of our land, where we'd never dared to step before. And then . . ." Gullinda coughed, and rubbed her eyes. "I saw my chance to save myself. Ramos had frightened me so much that I tucked a knife into my apron. I used it to hack at the many green fingers that held the beanstalk to the brink of our world. The vine fought to hold on like an animal, but at last I severed it completely. I only hope the boy made it safely down before it fell."

Nick's jaw hung open, and he almost laughed aloud. *While Jack was taking an ax to the bottom, the giantess really made it fall by cutting away the top!* He had a powerful urge to tell her everything he knew, but decided it would be wiser to stay quiet for the moment. *"The fate of your world . . ."* she'd said. What was that supposed to mean?

Gullinda sniffled. "After Ramos was gone, I knew peace for a while. But it did not last, because soon his two sons were born. And my troubles began anew.

"I hoped those boys would turn out better-natured than their father, but my hopes were dashed. I raised them the best I could, but they grew up wild and evil-tempered.

"I gave them good, gentle names. One I called Gallinor. The other Bellidor. But as soon as they were able, they chose their own names and forbade me to use the ones I had given them. They called themselves Gnasher and Basher. Bellidor—that is, Basher—is the one you hear sleeping now." Nick listened. Thankfully, the thunderous snoring continued.

"Basher is slow of wit and strong of body. He can pull deeply rooted trees right out of the ground. And his appetite matches his strength. A boy like you? Basher would finish off a score in one meal and still look for more."

"But as horrible as Basher is, Gnasher is worse. He is a weakling next to his brother, but fiercely smart. I had hopes for him—that he would be wise enough to learn good from evil. I taught him to read and to write. He yearned to know *everything*. And when he wanted me to teach him something, he was as sweet as could be." The giantess shook her head and smeared away some tears with the back of her wrinkled hand.

"It twisted my heart when I realized the truth: His sweetness was a fraud. He only was kind when he needed something. In truth Gnasher was just as wicked-hearted as his brother. Every bit of knowledge I gave him, he would put to evil purpose. The lessons about love and kindness he discarded.

"Gnasher began to create things. Little devices out of wood and rock and rope and iron. The first were just toys to play with, carts on wheels, and other amusements. But soon he moved onto larger ideas. Some of his devices were marvelous and useful. But most were awful, devious things. Traps were his favorite—traps to kill or maim any poor animal that wandered into them.

"As time went on, my sons grew worse. They mocked me and grew furious when I refused to do their bidding. They ate like animals and threw down their empty bowls, shouting at me to get more. Once again, I was no better than a slave.

"They destroyed anything that gave me pleasure. I grew a garden of flowers. The day it began to blossom, I found it trampled.

"Something broke inside me that day, and I did something I promised myself I never would do: I told them about their father. I don't know why I chose to do it at last. Maybe to make them think twice about treating me so cruelly. I never could have guessed what a mistake it would be to tell them, what pain and suffering it would cause."

The giantess looked at her hands. The fingers were cracked and thick with calluses. There were scars upon scars.

"I told them of their awful father, the boy Jack, and

the world of little people that Jack came from. And I told them about the great beanstalk that connected our worlds, and how I'd destroyed it to rid myself of Ramos.

"You should have seen the look on Gnasher's face. The wonder, the hunger, the wanting—I saw it all in his expression. 'Mother, tell us about this world of the small,' he said. He tried to sound kindly, but I knew sly Gnasher too well. I refused to say more. But I already had told him enough.

"For months after that, I did not see much of Gnasher. He would sit quietly in his room. Or he would wander off into the wild. Sometimes he would bring home a sack full of something and lock himself away.

"Whenever I saw Gnasher, he was deep in thought. You can tell when he's thinking from the way he twitches that nose from side to side.

"One day Gnasher took me by the hand and brought me to the treasure room. He said there was something I had to see. And like a fool, I believed him. As soon as I was inside, the door slammed behind me and I was locked in. Gnasher stood outside, laughing. He shouted through the door that I would still get a surprise, but it wasn't ready yet. He said this would be his greatest invention ever, and he had me to thank for the idea."

The giantess paused and settled back to rest against the pile of beanstalk matter. Nick did not know exactly where this story was going, but the uneasy feeling in his belly had turned to icy dread.

"I was a prisoner in that treasure room for a long, long time. There was nothing to do but listen to the odd sounds coming from the other side of the hall—from the room we sit in now," Gullinda continued. "This was not always a prison, you know. Before Gnasher and Basher were born, these were the stables for my cows and sheep. I raised them for milk and wool. But Gnasher and Basher had no patience for that. They slaughtered and ate them all.

"As I listened from the treasure room, I heard the cutting of wood and the hammering of nails. At times I caught the scent of smoke, and I knew that Gnasher was at his forge, where he made things of iron.

"Then at last the noises ceased and the door to the treasure room opened. Gnasher and Basher each took me by an arm and brought me here. The stables were gone, and the windows and doors were sealed with stone. I saw this strange machine that Gnasher designed, and in the middle of the room, a great heap of plants.

"Gnasher said, 'Do you see those vines, Mother? Those innocent vines that grow everywhere in our land? You would never guess what power they contain! Inside there's a fiber, Mother. Twine that fiber, and you get a powerful thread. Twine that thread, and you get a powerful string—strong enough to lift you off the ground! And do you know what you get when you twine those strings, Mother? The longest, strongest rope in the world, that's what!' Gnasher threw his head back and laughed again. Basher just ran around bellowing and thumping his chest.

"Gnasher was giddy with excitement. 'The rope is for the invasion, Mother,' he said. 'Basher and I, we're going down to the land of the little people. We'll take anything we want, and we'll crush anyone who stands in our way! They'll send their puny armies out to defy us, but we'll stomp and smash and slice their little soldiers. In time they will bow to us. They will sacrifice their young and weak to feed us. We'll rule as kings!'"

Nick's face grew pale at the thought of those man-eating monsters loose in the world below. How many would die under their feet and disappear down their throats? He had a horrible vision of the ogres rampaging through a village, tearing the roofs off of homes and snatching up the cowering people, devouring some on the spot and filling their sacks with the rest. . . . Nick shook his head, trying to clear the nightmarish image from his mind.

"Gnasher told me, 'You're going to weave the rope for us, Mother. See, I've built a machine to make the work go faster.' And he led me toward that infernal invention of his.

"I refused. I told him he was mad. But they locked me here with no food and water, and at last I had no choice but to do what they asked if I wanted to stay alive."

Nick looked at the strange contraption along the wall. "How does it work?"

"Like all of Gnasher's machines, his rope-weaver is ingenious. I first had to comb the fibers out from the vines that Basher brought me. The fibers went into those little holes around the first set of wheels. Gnasher's wind machine turned the wheels, and the fibers were spun into thread. The next wheels spun the threads together. The further down the line it went, the thicker the cord grew, until the final, largest wheels spun out the rope.

"But at first, Gnasher wanted only a single thin strand. For a long, long time, through darkness and light, I went on weaving that strand for him. And when he thought it was long enough, he took it to the edge of our land and lowered it, with a hook and a bucket tied to the end to see what they might bring up. Six times he thought it was long enough to reach the world below, and six times he returned to order me to make it longer.

"On the seventh try, he did it. When they reeled the rope in again, the bucket was full of strange water that tasted of salt. But all that mattered to Gnasher was that he succeeded. He knew his plan would work.

"Then he ordered me to weave a great rope, made up of many strands, to deliver them to the world below. How I cried when he said that. I was imprisoned for so long already, and yet my work had hardly begun. But I had no choice. I could either do what Gnasher said or be left here to die.

"As I finished the rope, Gnasher had me push it through that hole in the wall so he could measure it. He would inspect it as well, to be sure I did not purposefully weaken part of the rope. Believe me, if I could have gotten away with it, I would have.

"And I tell you, Nick, that rope can do what he wants it to do. It couldn't be stronger if it was spun from iron."

All this time the giantess had been toying with a piece of the beanstalk vine. She suddenly dashed it to the ground.

"Now the job is done. Gnasher said they would free me when the rope was finished. But have they? No! Gnasher says he cannot trust me, that I might destroy the rope, because I take pity on the lowly creatures below us! They will leave me here to perish." The giantess rolled over and buried her face in the pile to muffle her cries.

Nick wanted to comfort her, but he did not know where to begin. He looked away and noticed the end of a slender piece of string sticking out from the heap of beanstalk shreds. It was a stray thread from the great rope. He pulled on it, and more emerged from under the pile. As Gullinda cried, he absentmindedly wound it up. By the time the other end appeared he had a fist-sized ball of string. He stuffed it into his pocket as Gullinda finally raised her face. Her gray eyes were red-rimmed. She looked at the prison door.

"I tried to raise them well, to be better than their father," she said. "But in the end, nothing I did made a difference. There was something corrupting them from the inside. And it was stronger than I was."

There was a painful silence. Nick thought about what the giantess said a few minutes earlier: *The job is done.*

"Gullinda, did you mean that the rope is really finished? That they are going to use it?"

"It is ready. They are making the final preparations for their invasion. That road you heard Gnasher speak of is the one that will bring the rope to the edge of our world."

"But it doesn't seem possible," Nick said. He tried to imagine the size of the finished rope. "A rope that long— wouldn't it snap under its own weight?"

"You do not understand," said Gullinda. She looked at the floor and found a thick scrap of the rope lying nearby. She held it out over Nick. It was brown and green in color, seven feet long and a foot thick.

"Catch it, and you will see," the giantess said. She let it drop.

Nick gave a cry of surprise as it plopped across his waiting arms. He expected the weight of an ordinary rope, but this thick piece was light as a feather. "It can't be," he said, looking at it closely, as if searching for the missing pounds.

"There is something wondrous about these plants that grow here," Gullinda said. "And the fiber that comes from them is as strong as it is light. The rope will not break. Soon my sons will use it to descend on your world. And I made it possible."

"What else could you have done?" said Nick.

The giantess did not respond. She only sat there, a tormented look on her face.

The imminence of the invasion was a stunning conclusion to Gullinda's awful story. Nick felt like he could not breathe. He wanted badly to get out of that room, if even for a moment.

"I want to see the rope," Nick said hoarsely.

"It's on the other side of that hole," said the giantess. She pointed to the gap, just above the floor, into which the finished rope had been fed. It was a small opening to her, but to Nick, it was big enough to duck through without touching the sides.

Nick rose and stepped toward the hole. "I'll be right back."

"Will you?" asked Gullinda. She was looking at him now. A single tear, big enough to fill a goblet, rolled off her cheek and splattered by Nick's feet.

He struggled to smile. "Yes—to help you get out."

Gullinda turned her face away.

"You'll see," said Nick. He went through the hole.

He had passed through the back wall of the castle, into a kind of courtyard. A wooden roof had been assembled high overhead, projecting from the castle wall to protect the rope from the elements. But it was not just the rope that astonished Nick. It was also the vehicle that would transport the rope to the edge of the cloud island, and the machinery that was designed to lower it.

Like the strand Nick had examined, the great rope was brown and green, the color of a sapling. It was wound around a spool of staggering width and length. The spool was lying on its side atop a flat platform, which rode on four wheels that each looked as big as the moon. The end of the rope was threaded through a cog-and-wheel mechanism that jutted from the side of the platform. Other materials were piled behind the spool: spikes, chains, and hammers.

In front of the wagon, a bar stuck out, with a crosspiece at the end. It was meant for the ogres to each grab a side of the crosspiece, and haul the platform and spool behind them.

One look convinced Nick that the ogre's diabolical plot could succeed, after all. Worse yet, everything looked ready to go. The invasion was about to begin.

He felt helpless. All he had wanted from this strange place was something of value to steal, something to buy him a better existence than the bleak one he knew. So why did there have to be this terrible plot and that poor giantess to complicate everything? It made him angry to think about it—angry at Gullinda, just for existing.

What can you do about all this? Nick thought. *Nothing. You can't do anything for Gullinda; she'll end her days in that prison, whether you try to help her or not. And you can't foil this invasion. In a few days the world below will never be the same. You might as well get that sack of treasure and run. And* don't stop running until you're too far away for even the ogres to get you.

Go on. You can't make a difference here. Take the treasure first—you'll need it to survive. Take it and go.

Nick turned and whispered to the hole in the wall. "I'm sorry."

And then he ran.

• CHAPTER 15 •

Nick ran away from the rope, away from Gullinda. He circled around the rear wall of the castle and came upon a back door. It was smaller than the front entrance. When he slithered beneath it, he emerged into a hallway. It looked to be the distant end of the corridor that led from the great hall to the prison and treasure rooms.

Just inside the door, benches twenty feet high lined both walls. Nick saw handles and blades sticking out over the edge. Weapons for the invasion.

Farther down, hanging from pegs on the wall, Nick saw two suits of cloth armor, tailored to fit the ogres. The material was woven from the same green-brown fiber that created the rope. Worn in battle, it would be as strong and hard to penetrate as metal, without weighing the ogres down as they wielded their weapons. Gnasher and Basher would be nearly invincible.

Nick didn't want to think about the havoc the ogres would wreak with those weapons and that armor. He ran past the tools of war, down the corridor, and soon came to the treasure room door. He slid through the tight space near the hinges and picked up the sack. He took another look around the room and marveled at the riches all around him, regretting that he could carry so little. There would be no second or third trip; one would have to do.

As he turned to leave, he saw the figurine in the corner.

It was still covered by the cloth, but Nick didn't have to see it to remember the final shape that the object assumed. It was the way he looked right now, skulking away with a fortune on his back. In fact it was precisely the same pose.

Nick wobbled where he stood, and the skin on his arms turned to goose flesh. He lost his grip on the sack of treasure. It slid off his back and hit the floor with a muffled clatter.

What was this wicked object? All he'd felt when he touched it were the terrible urges he'd come to know too well. Greed. Violence. Vengeance. Regret. Despair.

But there was more to him than that. *Wasn't there?* There had to be.

He ran to the figurine and tore the cloth away, flinging it into the air behind him where it fell like a dying ghost. "You don't know me!" he yelled into the face. "This isn't me!"

But it was. It was what he'd become. A thief and nothing more. The dark magic of the figurine had revealed a truth to him. There were two kinds of thieves in the world: thieves like Jack, good people who succumbed to temptation, and whose conscience forever punished them for it; and thieves like Finch, predators who could murder and rob without a pang of regret. They were the haunted and the hunters. To one you gave your pity, to the other your contempt, and to neither your envy.

He stared into the shameful face of his likeness.

"What are you, really?" he asked aloud.

What I've become? Or what I might become?

"I'm back," said Nick, rising to his feet inside the prison room door.

When Gullinda turned and saw him, her face seemed to glow. "I would not have blamed you if you left."

"I'm here to help you escape," said Nick. "Maybe we can ruin their plan."

She smiled and shook her head.

"I would gladly help you do that, Nick, but there is no way for you to get me out of this room."

"But what about the lock? I could get the key," said Nick.

"I told you already. There is only one key. Gnasher wears that around his neck, with the keys to the treasure room and his own room, at all times."

"But when he falls—"

"And he sleeps lightly," Gullinda interrupted. "You could never remove it without him awakening. Never."

"Then I will stay, and bring you food and water."

"What a boy you are. Would you save one old woman instead of warning all your people? Go back down your beanstalk, Nick. Tell them the sons of Ramos are coming."

"I won't leave you here!" Nick kicked the pile of beanstalks and cried out in frustration. Then he turned to Gullinda with a strange look on his face. He started nodding to himself.

"He can read, can't he," said Nick. "You taught him to read."

"I did," agreed the giantess.

"Is there something to write with in this castle? And parchment, something to write on?" asked Nick, his voice quickening.

"Gnasher keeps those things in his room, so he can draw his inventions." The giantess wrinkled her brow, not understanding what the boy was getting at.

"Tell me where his room is," said Nick. "I know how to get you out of here!"

Nick crept forward as quickly as he dared, picking his way over the junk that was strewn all over the floor of the great hall. As he passed the arching entrance to the kitchen, he looked inside. Basher was still asleep by the table. Nick paused briefly to take a closer look at the monster.

Basher had dozed off at first with his head on the table. But now he leaned back in his chair, chin to chest, head lolled to one side. The ogre smelled like spoiled meat. His mouth hung open as he snored. A stream of pinkish drool oozed out of his mouth and snaked down his chest. A thousand flies swarmed over the bloody remains of the boar, and hundreds more flew around the ogre's face. Every time Basher drew in a great breath, a few unlucky bugs were sucked down his throat and up his nose. They didn't come out again.

Looking at the ogre made Nick queasy. He moved on through the great hall, into the corridor on the other side, toward the room that the giantess described. He knew he was running out of time. Gnasher would return from his errands soon.

The corridor twisted and turned like a creek. Along the way, Nick found a few dead rats on the floor. They were as flat as parchment, their bones crunched into dust, their legs splayed in odd directions. The ogres must have stepped on them with as little regard as Nick would have for an ant.

A broken chair was lying on its side against one wall. As Nick approached it, he glimpsed another large spider web, like the one he encountered in the crevice outside the castle. The spokes and spirals of the web were sewn between the chair's splintered legs. Behind that, a dark tunnel of silk curled back out of sight. Nick circled widely around the chair, hugging the opposite wall. He couldn't resist a closer peek at the web as he passed. Then he wished he hadn't looked.

This spider-head was female, with the face and the tangled gray hair of a hag. She sat high in the web, holding four dangling threads that dropped nearly to the floor, as if operating some invisible marionette. When she saw Nick, her eyes twinkled and she mewled to him in a chilling singsong voice. She lifted one leg and gestured with a tiny finger to come closer.

"No, thanks," said Nick. He looked at the floor beneath the web. The parched body of a male spider-head lay on its back there. Its eyes were rotted away, and its legs were curled above it.

A rat of ordinary size darted out from a crack in the wall in front of Nick. It was startled to see him and scampered to the other side of the corridor, too close to the dangling threads. The spider-head gave one thread a skillful snap, and it whipped into the rat and stuck fast. The rodent twisted and squealed as the drooling spider-head reeled it up to her perch. She nipped it on the back, and the rat went limp.

Nick was filled with loathing. He found a little stone and flung it at the spider-head. It missed to one side and stuck in the silky funnel. The spider-head glared at him, then laughed shrilly. Then she turned and called into the dark recesses of the web.

Within seconds, dozens of smaller forms crawled out of the shadows: baby spider-heads. They scuttled to their mother, and the first to arrive swarmed over the rat. The rest gathered around and bawled when they could not get their share. A few of them saw Nick standing on the other side of the hall. They cooed like infants and began to crawl down the web to the floor.

Nick decided it was time to move on.

Up ahead on the right, a second corridor branched off from the main passage.

"Don't go that way," the giantess had warned him. *"Basher's room is there. The smell alone would kill you."*

The giantess was hardly exaggerating. Even though he'd grown used to the awful odor that permeated the castle, Nick was not prepared for the tidal wave of stench that surged from that corridor. He put the crook of his elbow across his nose and ran past it, his eyes stinging. As he went by, he heard a low hum: the sound of a million buzzing flies.

Not far beyond that the corridor ended at the door to Gnasher's room. A lock hung from it as Gullinda predicted. Gnasher allowed no one in his room, not even his brother. Nick slipped like a mouse through the crack under the door, into the awesome tower room that Gnasher claimed for his own.

Standing there was like being inside a volcano. It was oppressively hot. Gnasher had built his forge here, where he hammered and molded the metal parts for his contraptions. A fire smoldered inside, casting red-black shadows that flickered on the walls. This was the source of the thin black smoke that Nick saw when he approached the castle. Giant hammers, tongs, and other smith's tools leaned against the walls of the forge, and a great black anvil stood nearby.

A wide staircase spiraled along the walls to the top of the tower. High overhead, Nick saw the inner workings of the wind machine. Through a window he could see the sails in motion outside, driven by the breeze. They turned a shaft that came into the tower through a hole in the wall and drove an assortment of meshing gears and rods. Ropes and chains were attached to the machinery in various places. Some disappeared into holes, on their way to power inventions throughout the castle. Others came straight down to drive ingenious devices inside the tower.

The power of the wind machine worked the bellows that blew into the furnace. The bellows moved up and down like an accordion, filling the tower with a living sound like deep, rhythmic breathing.

Elsewhere the power of the wind machine piped water up from a stone well in the center of the room. Inside the pipe, a screw turned, and water was drawn along its threads and trickled out of the top. The trickle fed a deep pool of water, where Gnasher could cool his newly forged metal creations.

Near the pool stood a table. On its top were several cages, filled only with chalky bones draped with ragged pelts. A long bench against the wall was covered with the tools of experimentation: crucibles and scales, and cups and spoons for measuring.

Hanging on the walls were sketches of inventions, drawn with black chalk on huge sheets of tan parchment. The largest drawing, twenty feet wide, showed how the rope would lower the ogres to the world below.

In the picture, the cart was parked at the edge of the cloud island and secured by stakes and chains. Gnasher was sitting in the harness and had just been lowered over the edge. Basher was watching Gnasher go.

Gnasher was a skilled artist, Nick had to admit. With a few simple strokes, he'd captured the ugly essence of Basher. Even the self-portrait was accurate.

Nick admired Gnasher's ingenuity until he saw another picture that reminded him of the ogre's demon nature. On the upper half of that parchment was the design for a weapon. It looked like the scythes that farmers used to harvest grain, with a long crescent blade that would sweep low across the ground. In the bottom half of the parchment, Gnasher had illustrated the weapon in use. A crowd of people was running from Basher. He was using the scythe to cut a bloody swath through the crowd.

The brutal drawing shook Nick out of his reverie. He quickly found the items he needed. A stub of chalk had fallen to the floor where Gnasher did his sketching. Nick grabbed it, blessing his luck that he did not have to climb onto the table.

One of Gnasher's smaller sketches hung close to the floor. Nick jumped and caught the bottom of the parchment. It tore away from the thin nails that held it to the wall and came off in his hands. Nick rolled it up so it would be easier to carry.

He shoved the chalk and the parchment under the doorway, then slid himself under. With the chalk in one hand and the parchment tucked under the other arm, he ran back down the hall.

Nick stopped abruptly as he came to the web of the spider-head. Her children, one hundred or more, littered the floor of the hallway, scrambling in every direction, crying in their tiny baby voices. The smallest had heads the size of apples, and some were several times that size. The skin on their hairless heads had a sickly complexion, a mottle of pinks, grays and purple bruises. Not all had eight legs—some had as few as three, and some scrabbled on too many limbs to count easily.

One of the swarm saw Nick and gave a happy squeal. The little thing seemed delighted to see him, but Nick was thoroughly revolted. As it scuttled close to his feet, he jumped over the outstretched arms. The baby spider-head cried out in frustration, and the rest of the brood turned to see what had happened. When they saw Nick coming, they all began to run toward him on their stilt legs. Staying close to the far wall, Nick raced ahead of the main pack, but at least seven more were between him and the way out. He kept running, darting left and right to avoid them. As disgusting as these creatures were, he didn't want to step on one of those heads. He could not stomach the thought of a skull cracking under his foot like an egg. The mother screeched at Nick from the web overhead in some shrill language he could not understand.

The babies were enjoying the chase. They giggled as they tried to catch him. The larger ones could spring to alarming heights, and Nick batted one away with the roll of parchment before it could latch onto his shirt.

Finally Nick sprinted past the last of the creatures. When they realized that their quarry had gotten away, the whole brood began to bawl. They ran back to the web and crawled up to the mother. She shooed the wailing babies back into the shadowy depths of the silk tunnel.

Nick continued on to the end of the hallway and saw Basher still snoring in the kitchen. The clever brother had not yet returned. Nick looked through the open front door to see if Gnasher was approaching, but another cloud was passing over the land and everything outside was smothered in fog. He ran across the great hall to the opposite corridor, to the prison room where the giantess waited.

Nick handed the giantess the rolled parchment. "Here. Rip it in half."

The giantess unrolled the paper and looked at Gnasher's sketch. It was the design for a weapon, a kind of crossbow that could sling a hundred arrows with a single shot. "It looks as if Gnasher has conjured up something special for his coming invasion. Such a waste of the mind he was granted," she said, shaking her head. She tore the parchment with gusto. "I'm glad to destroy this one. Let us hope he has not built it already."

Nick shuddered at the thought of that weapon being used on his countrymen. It looked like it could wipe out half of an army in a matter of seconds.

"Quick," he said. "Let me tell you what to write."

● CHAPTER 16 ●

Jack peered again over the crest of the hill at the abandoned farm below. It looked so much like the scrappy hut he shared with his mother long ago; it once sat on the same site where his fortress now sat.

Henry should have returned by now. Jack was growing anxious, hoping his faithful servant was not in danger.

Roland, the youngest of Jack's servants, interrupted the silence. "Master Jack, I want to tell you something."

"What, Roland?"

"Despite everything I've seen in the castle—the paintings, the hen, the golden eggs—part of me never really believed your story was true. I'm sorry."

"Don't be sorry. I have often wished it *wasn't* true," replied Jack.

"But I never knew . . . the reason for your sadness. . . ." Roland stammered, unable to find the words. Jack understood what Roland was trying to say anyway. His servants must have been tempted to ask, but none ever dared. But now all of them were humbled before the mighty beanstalk. It made them feel less like servant and master, and more like brothers, bonded by an extraordinary experience.

"Roland, you have a young man's lust for adventure. And you can't fathom why someone who has lived the greatest adventure of all, who climbed to a hidden world and won a fortune and killed a giant, cannot live happily for the rest of his days."

Jack turned his face toward the cloud above. "I'll tell you why. Her name was Gullinda," he said. "She found me on her doorstep and took me in. She fed me—kept me hidden from the giant, Ramos. And all she wanted from me was friendship—someone to talk to besides that devil that ruled over her. And talk we did, for hours and hours.

"She loved me, I think, like a son. And how did I pay her back? By stealing from her house. Three times I went back, and three times I stole. First I took a sack of gold while Ramos slept. The next day I returned—and Gullinda forgave me, so desperate was she for a kind companion! And for the second time I betrayed her, this time stealing the hen.

"Soon, even though I had an endless source of wealth, greed sent me back once more. This time I crept in without letting her see me. I watched Gullinda from hiding. She was weeping, and I could see that her husband had lost his temper when his precious hen had vanished and she could offer no explanation."

Jack was still staring at the vast black underbelly of the cloud. His voice dropped to a whisper, and Roland and Bill edged closer to hear him better.

"I should have turned around right then. Gone home and cut down that accursed plant. But I saw the harp at the sleeping giant's feet. And I *wanted* it. I wanted the thrill of taking it.

"I was creeping toward the door with the prize when I saw Gullinda staring at me. Her mouth was open, as if she was about to call to her husband. But she couldn't do it. Three times I had betrayed her, and she still wouldn't do anything to harm me.

"I could see the heartbreak on her face. I can see it now. I can see it always, when I close my eyes. And I can hear her whispering: *'Get out, Jack! Run away!'*

"It was the last time I ever saw her, because Ramos suddenly burst from his chair, where he only pretended to sleep. He'd set a trap for me—and heard Gullinda call me by name.

"I heard Ramos curse his wife. And then I heard things breaking. And that was all I knew, because I was running away as fast as I could."

Jack turned his face from the cloud and squeezed his eyes shut. He felt like there was a fist around his heart. He gritted his teeth and went on talking.

"And then he came down the beanstalk for me. And I nearly brought horrible destruction down upon all mankind." The old man buried his face in his hands.

Roland and Bill looked at each other helplessly.

Jack raised his head to meet their eyes. Having revealed this much, he decided to reveal it all. "And this is what I have lived with all these years. Brave as I was to steal the treasure, I was too afraid to go back and see what my thievery had done to the giant's wife. Did Ramos kill her before chasing me? I was too cowardly to find out—even though I always had the means to do so," he said, waving toward the beanstalk.

"I waited and waited. Do it tomorrow, I thought. Next week. Next month. Next year. A few times I even brought those beans out. Even dug the hole! But I was afraid. Weak. And one day, I woke up, and I was old. Just like that.

"But I had those beans to remind me of my shame, year after year. And then last night, that boy came to my house. That little thief, climbing up to steal my gold . . ."

"And you found a way to go back up there without really going back up there," Roland said.

Jack nodded. He tried to speak again, but his legs went weak and he began to fall. Roland caught him and put his hand behind the old man's head, and Jack buried his face in the young man's chest.

"Master Jack. Henry's coming," said Bill.

Jack lifted his head to watch Henry approaching along the ridge. When Henry arrived, the old man greeted him with a hug and thumped him on the back. Henry glanced over at Roland and Bill, surprised by Jack's affection. The two men just shrugged.

"It's them, all right. The gang from the forest. But no sign of the boy," said Henry. "They've made themselves at home in the old farmhouse, and they've got a little campfire going. They seem nervous, like they're waiting for something to happen. Rather like us."

"What shall we do, Master Jack?" asked Roland.

"Wait for now. Keep an eye on the beanstalk. And be prepared for anything," said Jack.

They waited in hiding, the boy and the giantess. They could not see each other, but her hand was by his side, and Nick sensed her trembling. Neither made a sound for a long while, until Gullinda spoke quietly. "You don't have to stay for this. If it does not work, he will know someone is here. And he will hunt for you."

"But I want to be here. I want to know that you're safe."

"I'm afraid for you, Nick."

Me too, Nick thought, *for both of us*. He patted the enormous hand. "Then let me tell you something to amuse you. Quietly, though, in case Gnasher comes. Remember what you told me, about how you cut the beanstalk away, and made it fall?"

"I do."

"Jack thought *he* cut it down! When you were cutting the top, he was taking an ax to the bottom!" Despite the danger, he couldn't help but laugh aloud, and soon the giantess laughed with him.

After a time, a sobering thought came to Nick. As Gullinda's laughter faded, he told her. "The giant was killed, you know—Ramos—when the beanstalk fell." Nick wasn't sure how the giantess would react to this news. Then he heard her sigh, like a long, low gust of wind.

"I never meant to kill him, you see. I just did not want him to come back."

"I know," Nick said. And he waited for his words to sink in, for Gullinda to understand what else he'd just revealed.

There was a rustling sound beside him: Gullinda straightening up where she sat. "Hold on—you said *Jack* thought he cut the beanstalk down," she said. "Do you know him? Do you know what happened to the boy?"

"Yes, ma'am," replied Nick. "I've met him. He's a very old man now. I don't think we live as long as you giants."

Her voice grew soft. "What is he like now, this Jack?"

Nick considered the question before replying. "He is the saddest man that ever lived. He thinks about you and this place all the time. Something terrible happened to him when he came up here, and he's spent his whole life regretting it."

"Is that so," said the giantess. She thought for a while, humming to herself. "When you see Jack again, could you tell him something for me?"

"Yes, ma'am," said Nick, although he wasn't so sure that Jack wanted to see *him* again.

"Tell him I have not forgotten, but I have forgiven.

Waste not another day on sorrow, not another moment. Live happily, and be at peace." Nick smiled and said that he would.

Far away, they heard a loud, echoing crash, like the sound of wood hitting stone. *The front door slamming shut,* Nick thought.

"Gnasher has returned," Gullinda said coldly.

● CHAPTER 17 ●

Gnasher stood before the closed door. He had collected one animal from a trap, and slain another with a slingshot. A pair of strange antlers stuck out from the sack he carried over his shoulder.

He saw a piece of paper on the floor just inside the entrance. His name was written across the top—not the name he called himself, but the accursed name his mother had given him. His lip curled in a spontaneous snarl. Under his name was a message. Gnasher picked it up and read:

GALLINOR,
I have escaped from your prison.
See for yourself.
—Mother

Gnasher hurled the bag of game to the floor. He threw his head back and screamed. The shout echoed back and forth across the great hall, like a chorus of monsters.

Basher woke with a start. He tried to leap from his chair, but it toppled over backward and the ogre crashed to the ground among the discarded bones. He looked up, still groggy, to see Gnasher rushing at him.

"Lazy, loathsome fool! Mother got out! She escaped while you slept!" Gnasher slapped his brother on the head. Basher lifted his hands to ward off the next blow. Finally he lost his temper and struck back, putting his boulder of a fist into Gnasher's stomach.

Gnasher stumbled backward and fell. Basher got up and stood over his brother with his fist raised to strike again. He hissed at Gnasher, with his mouth open and his black tongue quivering.

Gnasher sat there panting, holding his bruised gut, and glared at Basher. "You would strike back at me? You oaf! Would you like it if I left you behind and went to the world below on my own?"

Basher lowered his fist. His lip began to tremble. Gnasher stood and smashed the note against his brother's chest.

"And after what you've allowed to happen, that's just what I should do!"

Basher began to bawl.

"Quit your whining," Gnasher growled. "Just follow me." Gnasher ran down the hall to the prison room, and his rueful brother followed.

When Gnasher reached the prison door, he saw that

it was still locked. He peered through the little square opening in the door. His mother was nowhere to be seen. He reached to his neck and pulled the chain that held the keys out from his shirt. After fumbling for the right key, he unlocked the door and kicked it in. It swung open wide and hit the wall with a clap of thunder that echoed inside the prison.

Gnasher put a finger to his lips, signaling for Basher to be silent as he followed. Then he strode into the middle of the room. He saw no holes in the walls, aside from the one that the finished rope was fed through. The gaps in the ceiling were unreachable. And there were no tunnels dug in the floor. The locked door was the only exit.

"So how did she get out?" Gnasher asked, scratching the scruff on his chin. His nose started to twitch.

Basher mumbled and pointed at something. Gnasher looked and saw a second note like the one he clutched in his hand. It was attached to the hook at the end of one of the ropes driven by the wind machine, and it bobbed up and down like bait on a fishing line.

Gnasher ran to it and ripped it off the hook. He read it aloud:

GALLINOR,
Your great plan is ruined.
See for yourself.
Farewell forever.
—Mother

"No! My rope!" Gnasher shrieked and dashed out of the room. Basher followed, whimpering.

In the prison room, all was still for a moment. Then a voice peeped from the pile of beanstalk plants. "They're gone. And they left the door open!"

The plants rustled, and Nick and the giantess emerged from inside the pile where they had buried themselves.

"Imagine that," said Gullinda, chuckling. "A little one like you outwitting clever Gnasher!"

"Go quickly now," said Nick. "Get away before they find you, or before Gnasher figures out that someone else put the note in the hall for you."

"But you must run too, little man."

"I will," said Nick. "After I ruin his plans for real."

"Let me help you."

"No! You've been a prisoner long enough. I don't want them to catch you again. I'm small enough to get away with it, though. They'll never know I was there."

Nick heard the ogres' voices outside the castle as they approached the rope.

"Please, Gullinda," Nick begged, "they might peek in the hole and see you. Just get away. Run to the other side of that mountain. Don't be afraid. Maybe it's a better place to live, with nice folk like you."

Gullinda nodded. Then she reached for Nick, moving slowly and gently. Nick raised his arms so she could take him by his sides. She lifted him high and brought him to her shoulder. The giantess hugged him tenderly and patted him on the back with the tips of her fingers. Her coarse hair draped over his face.

"I only wish my sons had been good boys like you," she said.

Gullinda put Nick down carefully and walked to the door. She turned and whispered one last thing. "Remember my message to Jack, if you meet him again." Then she was gone.

Nick ran to the hole that led to the rope. He pressed himself against the wall to one side of the gap so he would be out of sight if one of the ogres looked through. He could hear the monsters talking outside.

"Check it! Check every inch! Make sure she hasn't cut it anywhere," Gnasher's screechy voice ordered his brother.

Certain that the ogre's attention was not on the hole, Nick risked a peek. Basher was on the cart, climbing around the spool to inspect the rope. Gnasher paced around, mumbling and thinking, with a note clutched in each hand. His nose was twitching madly.

"But why would she bother to leave a note . . . and how did she get out of the locked room . . . and why would she risk leaving a note at all . . . ?" Something seemed to click in Gnasher's brain. He looked at the note clutched in his hand. Then he turned the parchment over, and saw his sketch on the other side. It was the sketch that could only have come from his locked room, where Gullinda never could have entered.

Gnasher's head snapped in the direction of the hole. Nick darted back to one side, unsure if he was seen. *He knows,* he thought. Nick heard Gnasher whisper something to Basher and then the sound of ogre footsteps running around the back of the castle. *And one of them is coming.*

Nick patted the pocket that held his knife, to make sure it was still with him. He brought his head slowly to the hole again. He had to get out of this room before Basher or Gnasher came in. But he also had to be careful that one of the ogres wasn't waiting, catlike, to pounce on the other side.

Before he could look out again, a powerful hand clamped on his shoulder. Another went across his mouth and cut off his scream. The hands spun him around, and Nick looked into the smiling face of Finch—the man who would travel any distance for revenge.

"I'm late to this party, Nick, but I'm sure you're happy to see me. It's been mighty entertaining, listening to you and that ugly old lady-friend of yours. Thank goodness she left, so you and I could have this chat."

Nick tried to yell something into the hand, but Finch shoved him back into the wall. Nick's head thudded against the rock, and his eyes lost focus for a moment.

"Don't interrupt me when I'm talking to you, boy. It's rude."

Finch kept Nick pinned against the wall with the one hand across his mouth. The other hand came up holding the jagged knife. He placed the tip of the blade under Nick's chin.

"Guess I owe you an apology, Nick. I was angry with you for running off on me. But it turns out you had the right idea after all. Never mind Old Man Jack's gold; you went straight to the source.

"I heard the old woman talk about the treasure room. And I tried to squeeze under that door, but I couldn't fit. So I need a little help from my young recruit. Make a few trips to that room for me, and maybe I'll forgive you for what happened at Jack's house. What do you say to that, Nick?" Finch took his hand off Nick's mouth so he could speak.

"*Run!*" Nick shouted, looking with wild eyes toward the door. Finch turned and saw the leering monster Gnasher at the entrance.

"So, there they are: mother's little assistants," said Gnasher. The ogre hunched over and put his hands close to the floor, with his long pointy fingers curved like talons. His lips curled back to expose sharp yellow teeth, and his eyes narrowed. Then he rushed at them with horrific speed.

Finch shoved Nick into the path of the ogre and ran. Nick stumbled and fell to the floor. Before he could get to his feet, Gnasher was on top of him. Nick sprang away as Gnasher snatched, but his ankle was trapped between two of the ogre's gnarly fingers.

Finch was heading for the hole in the wall when Gnasher lunged for him with the other hand. Finch sensed the claws coming and dove for the opening. Gnasher's nails scraped across the stone, but Finch was already through. He slid to a stop in the short tunnel that led outside.

Nick was hanging upside down in Gnasher's grip. He kicked at the hairy hand with his free foot. Gnasher ignored Nick and got to his knees to peer through the hole at Finch.

"Hello, little man," Gnasher said, baring his fangs. When Finch saw the wicked face at the entrance to the hole, he crammed his fist into his mouth, muffling his own scream. Gnasher stuffed his free hand into the opening. Finch turned and ran out the other side. But as he emerged, a larger hand crashed to the ground in front of him, a wall of pebbly, warty skin, and it appeared so suddenly that Finch ran into it before he could stop. Another hand came down behind, and the hands clapped together with Finch caught between. Only his head and the tops of his shoulders were sticking out above, and his legs dangled out underneath. He still held the knife, but he could not move his arm to wield it.

At first Finch was so startled he did not realize he was in the grip of a monster. Then he felt himself rising as Basher stood.

Basher, seeing and holding a human for the first time, grunted with curiosity. He lifted the man to his nose and sniffed deeply, closing his eyes as he enjoyed the scent of fresh, exotic meat.

Finch looked at that huge mouth and the awful rows of yellow teeth, some sharp for tearing and some blunt for crunching. He tried to squirm out of the ogre's grip, but he could do no more than wiggle in futility.

Basher was amused. The brutish ogre's mouth opened in a grin so impossibly wide that it threatened to continue past his ears and split the ugly head in two.

Finch screamed anew as Basher raised him up and opened his mouth wide. Then the scream sounded different because Finch was *inside* the mouth, and the lips had closed behind his head and across his shoulders. In that stinking wet blackness, he felt terrible teeth on both sides of his neck that began to press together.

Gnasher's voice came screeching through the hole in the wall. "Basher! I know you, pig! You better not be harming that one—I want to talk to him first!"

With a grunt of disappointment, Basher withdrew his prey from his mouth. Finch was not moving now, except for a barely perceptible trembling. His eyes stared into space, wide-open and unblinking, and his face was cold and pale. With a guilty look, Basher wiped Finch's head and shoulders across the fur of his vest, trying to clean the drool off before his brother arrived and learned what he'd been up to.

Inside the prison room, Gnasher passed Nick into his other hand, gripping him around the waist.

"Let me go! Put me down!" yelled Nick. He pummeled the ogre's hand with his fists.

"Put you down?" said Gnasher. "I ought to put you down my throat, for all the trouble you've caused, little morsel. Helping Mother escape—what a vexing, interfering breed you little folk are! But perhaps I should not be angry. After all, this is an opportunity to learn more about your kind before my brother and I descend on your world.

"Let's collect your friend, shall we? And then we can get to know each other in my room. So many questions spring to mind; I must have the answers."

Gnasher left the room and turned down the corridor to the castle's rear exit. He paused at the shelves full of weapons to allow Nick a good long look. "See them boy? Soon to be wielded on your people." The pride was evident in the ogre's voice.

Gnasher opened the door and stepped outside. He saw his brother prodding the man with his finger. The man's eyes were open, but he was not moving. Basher grinned sheepishly as Gnasher approached.

"What have you done, idiot? I told you not to harm him!" snapped Gnasher. He held out his open hand. Basher reluctantly gave up his prize. Finch fell limply into Gnasher's palm, still holding the jagged knife. Gnasher flicked it away with his fingernail. He brought Finch up for a closer look and shook him a little, but there was no reaction.

"Bah. He's not dead, just scared nearly to death." Gnasher turned to Nick. "Is he always such a coward? How come you don't seem so frightened?"

"I guess I'm used to being pushed around by stupid bullies, and he's not," Nick said.

Gnasher sneered. He raised Nick to the level of his mouth and made a purposeful display of his sharp yellow teeth. "Then come with me, my little morsel, and I'll invent new reasons to be afraid."

Gnasher turned back to his brother. "Basher! Stay by this rope until I return. *Don't* let me catch you sleeping this time. Understand?"

Basher nodded enthusiastically. He pointed at Nick and Finch and whined like a dog begging for scraps.

"Don't worry, you'll get your share," Gnasher said, "after I get my answers."

Gnasher went back in the castle. With Finch in one hand and Nick in the other, he crept softly along the corridor—as softly as an ogre could creep. When he reached the great hall, he peered around the corner and into the kitchen.

"Forget it, Gallinor. You won't catch her again," Nick said loudly, in case Gullinda was near.

Gnasher's lip curled on one side. "You give her too much credit."

The ogre went to the opposite corridor and headed for his room, the tower room. Even he held his breath as he passed the corridor that led to Basher's festering abode. When he reached his door, Gnasher put Finch on the floor. Finch lay on his back, staring up with glazed eyes, not moving. Just for safekeeping, the ogre used his toes to pin Finch to the floor. With his free hand, he reached inside his vest and pulled out a chain that held an assortment of keys, large and small. He used the largest key to unlock his door.

Gnasher picked Finch up again and stepped inside. "Welcome to my lair," he said to Nick, grinning. "Oh, I forgot—you've been here already, haven't you?"

Nick did not answer. Gnasher tightened his grip. Nick felt a great pressure on his ribs and the breath being squeezed from his lungs. He opened his mouth and tried to draw in air, but couldn't fill his lungs.

"You'll answer me when I pose a question, morsel," Gnasher said. Nick was still unable to speak, but he nodded. Gnasher relaxed his grip, and Nick gulped at the air.

Gnasher walked to the high table that stood near the center of the room. He put Finch and Nick down on its wide surface. "Move and I kill you. Understand?"

"Yes," Nick said in a raspy voice, rubbing his aching chest. Finch was still not responding.

Gnasher looked over his cages and selected the two with the narrowest gaps between the bars. With a pair of his smallest keys, he unlocked the doors. He shook the cages and dry white bones tumbled out, clattering musically on the tabletop. "I must take better care of my pets," the ogre said. He set the cages side by side.

"Now," he snarled at Nick. "Get in." He was pointing to the smaller cage.

Nick walked into the little jail. Gnasher grabbed the back of Finch's shirt between his thumb and finger and dragged the man inside the other cage. The ogre locked both doors and tucked the keys inside his shirt.

Gnasher lowered his face, inches away from the bars of Nick's cage. A demon grin bent the ogre's mouth. It was an expression calculated to frighten, but Nick refused to drop his gaze or step back as the ogre's hot, foul breath washed over him. His little fists clung tight on the cage's bars.

"I will give your friend a short time to recover," Gnasher said, "and then the questions begin. In the meantime, let's see if I can sniff out where Mother is hiding. I look forward to our next little chat, morsel."

Gnasher left the room and closed the door softly behind him.

Nick heard Gnasher lock the door from the other side. He slumped to his knees and rested his head against the bars.

Finch woke suddenly from his trance, screaming and thrashing on the floor of his cage. He rolled from side to side and punched at phantoms in the air.

Nick stood up and went to the side of the cage closest to Finch. "Finch! Stop it! Look at me, Finch!" he yelled, trying to make himself heard over Finch's hollers. A few of the animal bones were left on the floor of Nick's cage. He seized one and hurled it between the bars at Finch's cage. It struck the side loudly.

Finch looked around, and when he saw Nick, he stopped screaming. The man's eyes were huge. A strange, frightened smile emerged on his face. He started to laugh, a mad giggle that chilled Nick to the bone: "*Hee hee hee hee hee . . .*"

"Stop that!" said Nick.

Finch went on laughing. Nick threw another bone at him in disgust. It struck Finch on the shoulder, but it had no effect.

Nick wondered what he could say to get Finch to shut up. "The ogre will come back if you don't stop!"

That did it. Finch went silent instantly. His eyes darted around, taking in the amazing sights of Gnasher's room: the sketches, the inventions, the angry red forge, the heaving bellows, the dark pool of water in the center, and the grinding cogs and wheel of the wind machine high above.

"What is this place?" he said at last. His voice was hoarse from screaming.

"It's the ogre's room. Gnasher's room."

Finch pressed his face between the bars. "Gnasher? *Gnasher?* What's he going to do to us?"

"Ask us questions first. I don't know what happens then."

"They're going to eat us, aren't they? Aren't they!" Finch's voice cracked in fear.

Nick ignored the question. "Finch, is anyone else up here with you? Toothless or Squint?"

Finch squeezed his eyes shut and pounded his forehead against the bars. "I told them all to wait—that I'd deal with you myself."

"Will they come anyway, if you've been gone for long?"

"No. I told them to stay put until I returned. And they will."

Nick knew it was true. There would be no rescue—not that he could count on Finch's band for help after he'd betrayed them.

Gullinda could not get into this locked room to save him either. And besides, Nick truly hoped that she was miles away by now, on her way to a better life.

And Greeneyes? He didn't even seem real; it was folly to hope for him to intervene. He was just the mysterious figure who set events in motion and perhaps watched, amused, to see how things would come out in the end.

"This shouldn't be happening. I shouldn't be here," Finch muttered.

Nick couldn't believe how much he had feared this pathetic man a few hours before. Back then, he'd been afraid to look Finch in the eye. Now the villain lay curled up like a ball on the floor of his cage, and Nick could scold him like a child.

"No? Where should you be, Finch?"

"I should be a baron by now. In my own castle."

"So that's where you came from. What happened? Why aren't you?"

Finch was chewing at his fingernails, staring at nothing. "I . . . I had to run. They were going to hang me. Said I killed my brothers."

Nick shook his head. "But you did kill them, didn't you? Let me guess: because they were in your way."

Finch closed his eyes. "They were weak. They weren't worthy. It should have been mine, the barony."

So you went on the run and put together your nasty band, thought Nick. *And everything was fine until you followed me up the beanstalk.* The hair stood on Nick's neck when he remembered the beanstalk and the easy path it offered to the ground. Gnasher was no fool. He might realize that if people were here again, then a new beanstalk must have brought them.

"Finch! Listen to me!"

Finch opened his eyes and looked vacantly at Nick.

"Finch, we can't tell the ogres about the beanstalk, no matter what they do to us. We can't make it that easy for them to get down."

Finch's expression darkened. Suddenly Nick was staring back at the old Finch again, angry and cruel. "Listen to you, Nick. Always the hero. Such a good little boy. What a fool you are! You had the gold in your grasp, in Jack's house, but you decided to have an adventure. You had it again in this castle, but you decided to be the hero. And now look at you. Take a good look, boy, because this is how the real heroes end up: eaten alive, one way or the other."

Finch's words were like venom spreading in Nick's blood. He clapped his hands over his ears, but Finch only spoke louder.

"Are you proud of yourself, Nick? Because it's not just you that's doomed now! *You* summoned this infernal cloud. Now how many of your countrymen will suffer because of what you've done—crushed like beetles under their feet? Imagine the screams when they see the monsters coming, Nick. If only you could be there to witness it. And if only they could know who brought this suffering down on them. Your name, boy—they'd all die cursing your name: Nick, the thief who fancied himself a hero. Ha!"

"Shut your mouth!" Nick screamed at last. He flung another bone at Finch, but it clattered off the side of the cage. Finch threw back his head and laughed.

Nick curled up on the bottom of the cage with his back to Finch and drew his knees to his chest. It took all his resolve to make it this far, and suddenly there was nothing left inside. He needed arms to cradle him, but there were only bars around him. He needed warmth, but there was only cold iron and stone. He needed solace, but there was only the raving madman nearby.

His mouth opened in a soundless cry. Finch was

right: This was his own fault. There was nothing left to face but the return of Gnasher and whatever final horror that would bring. The room grew dim, and as Nick felt the sleep of exhaustion take him, he made a wish that he would never wake up.

⚜ CHAPTER 18 ⚜

Footsteps. Thumping, loud and heavy. The scratch of a key inside a lock, and hinges squeaking.

The sound seemed to go on forever, until at last there was the loud crash of wood against stone as the door to the tower room opened wide.

Nick willed himself awake from his deathly slumber and saw Gnasher at the door. The ogre stepped inside and locked the door again. Locking it against Gullinda—who else? Knowing that she was still free gave Nick a small measure of relief.

Gnasher came directly to the table. There was dark purpose in his stride.

Finch retreated to the back of his cage and clung to the bars. He cowered and moaned with fear as Gnasher lifted his cage.

"On your feet, I see. Found your courage yet, little man?" Gnasher gave the cage a shake. Finch did not respond; he only quivered and turned his face away from the ogre.

Still holding Finch's cage, Gnasher turned to Nick.

"And you, little morsel. Why, you look like you've been crying. You seem like such a tender child. And helpful. You certainly helped my mother. Is that what you like to do—rescue those in need?"

Nick sat in the corner of his cage and stared sullenly back at the ogre.

"Well, let's find out," Gnasher said, and he tossed Finch's cage high into the air. Finch screamed as the cage tumbled and splashed into the pool of water nearby. He pulled himself to the top to snatch a final breath of air, and then the cage sank under the surface. The ripples spread to the sides, returning to meet again in the middle. Nick's mouth fell open.

Gnasher pulled up a stool and slowly brushed dust off the seat. He sat at the table, leaning on one elbow.

"Don't do this," Nick said quietly.

"Don't fret, boy. This is another opportunity to be helpful. I'll fish him out as soon as you answer me: Where is the beanstalk?" The ogre folded his arms and smiled, waiting for the answer and savoring the moment.

Nick froze. How could he answer that question and bring swift and certain doom to the innocents below?

But how could he not answer the question? He looked at the pool of water and saw bubbles gurgle up and burst at the surface.

Nick needed a lie. A convincing lie. And he needed it fast. But nothing came to him. All he could think of was Finch in his cage at the bottom of that pool.

"The beanstalk is gone," Nick blurted. It was the first thing that popped into his head. He hoped he could find the right words to say next, the untruth that would convince the ogre not to seek out the mighty plant.

"So there *was* a beanstalk," Gnasher said, looking pleased with himself. "That is what brought you here, like the boy before you. Jack was his name, was it not?" Gnasher leaned back and casually examined his sharp fingernails, and waited for Nick to continue.

"Yes! We came up a beanstalk! But they must have cut it down."

"Who, morsel? Who cut the beanstalk down?"

Another cluster of bubbles, larger ones, floated from the depths of the pool. Nick pointed to the water. "Get him out. You said you would if I told you where the beanstalk was. And I told you—it's not here anymore. If you want to hear the rest, get him out now!"

Gnasher laughed. "Such a brazen child! Yes, I'll get him out, but only because I have questions for him as well." The ogre walked to the pool. He stuck his arm in, nearly to the shoulder. "Can't seem to find him," he teased, swishing his arm about. "Ah, here he is."

The ogre brought the dripping cage up, with Finch sputtering and coughing inside. Gnasher set it beside Nick's once more. Finch rolled onto his side and took great gasping breaths.

Nick trembled with fury as he saw the amused look on Gnasher's face.

"Now, morsel. Continue with your story."

"My name is Nick." He was stalling for time. A lie was forming in his head, and his mind raced as he tried to resolve it.

"Your name is not significant," Gnasher said, with a wave of his hand. "Only the beanstalk matters—where it came from, and what happened to it. Tell me now."

Nick was ready. Like the best lies, this one had just enough truth in it. "That man and I are thieves," Nick said. "A while ago, we robbed a fellow we'd never seen before, and got these beans he said were magic. Now, we'd all heard of this island in the clouds and the giants who live here. We thought people might come to cut down the beanstalk if we grew it, but we decided to take our chances. We wanted the treasure."

Gnasher sat with his head cocked to one side, absorbing every word. Nick realized with some alarm that Finch had recovered from his near drowning and was listening as well. The frightened man's eyes darted back and forth between him and the ogre. Finch clearly did not want to say anything to draw the ogre's attention. Nick hoped he'd stay that way.

"So we grew the beanstalk," Nick continued. "We just planted the beans and stood back, and up it went. The two of us climbed it and found this castle. My job was to slip under the door to the treasure room. I saw all the treasure you've got in there. I even touched that golden figurine. I guess you have too." Nick was pleased to see the smirk disappear from Gnasher's face at the mention of the figurine.

"So I brought out some treasure and gave it to this man, Finch. He carried it to the edge. But when he got there, the beanstalk was gone! Chopped down, while we weren't looking. We were trapped.

"So we came back and struck a bargain with your mother. We told her we'd help her escape if she would help us get back to our land."

Gnasher leaned back and folded his arms. "And how did she mean to return you to your land?"

"She said there was a narrow strand of the rope that she'd made, and she'd use it to lower us." Nick hoped the lie made sense.

Finch was watching uneasily to see how the ogre would react. He glanced at Nick, and Nick flicked his eyebrows up. *Don't ruin it, Finch,* he willed. *Play along.*

Nick saw Gnasher's nose begin to twitch. Something seemed to be troubling the ogre as he considered the story Nick had told. And that was when Nick remembered the flaw in his lie: *the sun.* A steady beam of late afternoon light was shining through the windows at the top of the tower. But if the cloud was not held fast by the beanstalk, that shaft of light should be wandering. The shadows should be dancing, as Gullinda put it.

Like a chess player who suddenly realized he'd left himself vulnerable to checkmate, Nick hoped that his opponent would not detect the weakness.

He decided to distract the ogre. "Why do you want to invade our world? You have everything you need right here."

A wicked light twinkled in Gnasher's eyes. "Do I really?" He got up from the stool and strutted around the room, making sweeping gestures. "What do you see here, morsel? What lies all about you in this room?"

Nick looked around him. "Lots of stuff."

"Lots of stuff, indeed," Gnasher sniffed. "Everything here is a testament! A testament to my genius. There is nothing I can't conceive, nothing I can't create.

"I have the wits of an emperor. But I lack an empire to rule. What is in this forlorn place, but my brother, weak of mind, and mother, weak of heart? What sort of kingdom is that for one so clever as me?

"That is why I was so intrigued by the story of the land of little people. There's a place worth conquering, I thought. And here I am, about to begin my invasion, and who should turn up but a lovely pair of specimens of the breed that shall soon bow down to me. How convenient—almost as if it was meant to be. Now I shall know what to expect when my brother and I arrive.

"You, obviously, are only a child. But you," Gnasher said, turning to address Finch directly, "look like a little warrior. Tell me how your people will defend themselves when we arrive."

Finch pressed himself against the back of the cage. He tried to speak but only stammered. Gnasher slapped at the top of the cage and Finch cringed.

"Speak up, vermin," Gnasher snapped. "You've spent some time in my pool. You'll bathe in the furnace next if you don't answer me now: How will your people defend themselves?"

"They'll . . . they'll run away at f-f-first," Finch said, "b-but then they'll g-gather into armies. They'll try to t-take shelter behind fortress walls."

"How high are these walls?"

"The b-biggest are as tall as you. None higher."

"How many are in these armies?"

"Hundreds. They m-might gather thousands for a great battle."

"All will die who confront us. Now tell me what weapons they will use."

The questions went on and on. Gnasher made Finch describe in detail the swords, spears, bows, and arrows that men would wield, the catapults that could launch heavy stones, and the methods that men employed to defend their fortresses from attack. The ogre inquired about the dwellings of common people and the livestock they kept. He asked where the wealth was stored. He asked about the nature of the world below, and was fascinated to hear that it was in fact a larger place than his own island in the clouds, and that endless bodies of salty water surrounded the land.

The inquisition ended at last when Gnasher heard the panicked cries of his brother. "Now what?" he muttered.

He hurried up the stairs of the tower room and leaned his head out of a narrow window at the top.

"What are you screaming about?" Gnasher called. Basher was still standing guard by the rope, but he was hopping about nervously and pointing at the center of the castle. Dark smoke streamed out of the cracks in the decaying roof over the great hall. "Fire? Stay where you are, brother! I'll see to the fire!" Gnasher came running down the steps.

"If this is her doing, you will suffer greatly before you die," the ogre said to Nick and Finch as he ran past. He opened the door to his room, then closed and locked it from the other side. They heard his footsteps drumming down the hall.

"See what your meddling has done!" Finch snapped. But Nick was in no mood to argue. Something had occurred to him.

"Listen, Finch, this is our chance to escape—maybe the only one we'll get," said Nick. "I watched you pick the lock on that trunk we stole—could you pick the locks on these cages as well?"

Finch stared back at Nick for a moment. Then he stood to examine the door. "Perhaps I can," he said quietly. He leaned over and reached under the bottom of his pant leg. He withdrew a smaller dagger, previously hidden, that was strapped to his ankle.

The keyhole on the door was set in the middle of a wide iron plate. Finch reached across the plate from one side, trying to use his dagger as a pick. He strained mightily for the dark rectangular opening, but only the tip of his knife could reach it.

"It's no use. It's too far. Curse it all, we're going to die!" he screamed. Then he turned his back to the bars and slid down to sit on the bottom of the cage.

"Finch!" called Nick excitedly. "Pick the lock on my door instead!"

Finch turned and looked at the distance between the two cages—four yards or more. He laughed grimly. "Oh, that's a fine idea, boy. But you're over there, and I'm over here. How do we bring these cages together?"

Nick stuck his hand in his pocket and produced the ball of string he'd collected when talking to Gullinda. "This is made from the same fiber as the beanstalk. It's strong enough to pull my cage to yours, and I think it's long enough." Without waiting for Finch's reply, Nick knelt at the side of his cage. Holding on to one loose end of the string, he lobbed the ball toward Finch's cage. It spanned the distance between them with many feet to spare. "See?"

Finch plucked up the end of the string and looked at it. The strand was so narrow it would have sliced into his flesh if he tried to grab it and pull. He picked up a bone and wound the string around it, while Nick secured the other end of the string to his own cage.

Bracing his feet against the bars, and gripping the bone on either side of the string, Finch pulled backward in a rowing motion, grunting loudly. Nick's cage did not budge.

"Wait! I can help," said Nick. He went to the opposite side of his cage and stuck his legs between the bars, ready to push with his feet as Finch pulled.

As Nick got into position, he happened to glance toward the door. Something familiar crept underneath into Gnasher's room. It was one of the baby spider-heads. The creature saw him and smiled broadly. With a squeal of delight, it turned around on its knobby legs and scooted under the door again.

"Uh-oh," said Nick.

"What is it?" said Finch.

"Never mind. Just *pull!*"

The smoke grew thicker as Gnasher approached the great hall, where small fires had been lit in several places. The ancient tapestries on the walls were ablaze, and the smashed pieces of furniture had been piled together and set aflame as well. Smoke rose to the ceiling, and twinkling cinders fell like snow.

"Mother!" snarled Gnasher.

The castle was built of stone, so the fire would burn out eventually. But still, Gnasher knew he must contain it before smoke filled every room and drove him from the castle. He pulled a tattered rug off the floor and used it to beat and smother the fires, one by one.

As Finch hauled on the strand and Nick pushed off the table surface with his feet, the cage slid forward several inches. Finch turned the bone in his hands, winding the string to take up the slack. Nick counted aloud, "one, two, three," again and again, and the cages inched closer with every pull. The color was back in Finch's complexion. In fact his face was bright red from the effort, and thick veins were embossed on his neck. At last the cages stood side by side, with the lock on Nick's cage within arm's reach of Finch.

Nick glanced at the door again. Dozens of little spider-heads had flooded underneath it into Gnasher's room. They came across the floor, heading directly for the table.

Finch gasped. "I saw those things—what are they?" A hint of hysteria was creeping back into his voice.

"Just pick the lock before they get here!" yelled Nick.

Finch stuck his hand into the keyhole first and probed with his fingers for a moment. A look of hope flashed across his face. "It's a simple lock—hardly a lock at all! A child could do it!" He looked over nervously as the spider-heads went out of sight under the tabletop. They were racing toward the corners of the table. The table legs, made from whole trunks of trees with the rough bark still on them, would be easy for them to climb.

"What are they going to do to us?" Finch shrieked.

"Forget the stupid spiders and open the stupid door!"

Finch slid the dagger into the hole. His hand was trembling, so he steadied it with the other hand. He probed inside the keyhole, and found the thing he was looking for—a pin that, when raised, would unbolt the door.

Nick could hear the *scritch-scratch* of spider feet on the legs of the table. He tried to ignore the sound and watched Finch carefully, knowing it would be his turn to unlock Finch's cage once he was free.

Finch wedged the blade against the edge of the keyhole for leverage, and twisted the blade to raise the pin. As frightened as Finch was, he still had the deft touch of a thief. Nick heard a click in the lock. He pushed on his door and it swung open, rusty hinges protesting, and struck the side of Finch's cage, leaving a gap just wide enough for him to slide through sideways.

"You did it!" cried Nick.

Finch was not celebrating. He stared aghast at the distant end of the long table and pointed with the knife. "Look!"

A single dark twiggy leg hooked over the corner of the tabletop, then two more, and the first spider-head hauled itself up. It stood there, propped on all eight limbs, with the bald baby head bobbing up and down in the center. The hideous thing was tuckered out from the climb. It panted, with its too-long tongue hanging from its fanged mouth and dribbling drool. It stared quizzically at Nick and Finch, unsure if it should approach them alone.

"Get me out!" screamed Finch, his words blurring together. "*Get me out, get me out, get me out, get me out!*"

"Give me your knife. Now!" said Nick. Finch slapped the handle of the dagger into Nick's hand. He ran around Finch's cage to the side with the door. But instead of picking the lock immediately, he stepped back out of arm's reach.

"What? What are you waiting for?" Finch screamed, in a voice hoarse from shouting.

"Promise you won't hurt me," Nick said.

"I promise! I swear! Now get me out! I'm begging you!"

"All right. Watch that thing for me, though." He put the tip of the knife inside the keyhole.

Finch shouted frantic instructions at him. "No, not there, the other side! Feel around for the little pin—it's like a lever you have to lift—and get the knife under it! Have you got it? Now push down on the handle to force it up, and turn the blade as you push—that's right! *Look out behind you!*"

Gnasher snuffed out the last of the fires in the great hall. Only a few harmless piles of embers were left. Those would die on the stone before long.

But why was the smoke still growing thicker? Gnasher raised his nose and sniffed. He saw smoke running like an upside-down river along the ceiling of the corridor to the rope-weaving room. If that room was on fire, full as it was with the dry shreds and husks of the vines, there would be no putting it out. He would be lucky to retrieve his armor and weapons from the end of the corridor.

Gnasher threw back his head and howled, rapping his fists against his skull.

Enough of this. It was time to leave this place. Just one more trip back to his room to collect the prisoners—he would still have his revenge on them for releasing his mother. And then, let the conquest begin.

Nick whirled around to see the spider-head rushing at him, its legs clattering across the surface of the table. Its fangs were bared and its gaze was fixed on his ankle. He drew back his foot and kicked savagely at the thing as it went for his other leg. There was a satisfying thud as he struck it hard, right under the chin. The creature didn't weigh much—the head felt as light and hollow as a dry gourd—and it flew up and tumbled in the air before landing on its back a good distance away. The spider-head howled and its skinny legs went wild, scratching at air as it scrambled to right itself. It limped in a circle with its eyes crossing and rolling. Then it wandered too near the edge and blundered off. A second later there came a sickening sound, like the splat of rotten fruit on the stone floor below.

"The lock! Get the lock before more—" began Finch, and then he cut off his own words with a strangled, frightened screech. Nick looked to the end of the table. Dozens more of the disgusting things had mounted the tabletop. Now they waited quietly at the far corners, their numbers amassing as the slower members of the brood reached the top. The early arrivers stood high on their legs, bobbing in place to separate rhythms, whispering to each other in shrill voices that made Nick's flesh crawl. With every passing second, another one or two climbed over the side and joined the swarm.

There were at least fifty now, enough to overwhelm the man and the boy. They advanced cautiously, fanning out across the width of the table as if following some unspoken battle plan.

"The lock!" screamed Finch. *"Open the lock, the lock, the lock, the lock, the lock!"*

Nick slid the knife back inside the keyhole. For a moment, he couldn't remember what to do. The horde was halfway there. They were getting bolder, coming faster. Their whispers grew fiercer, and some giggled with excitement.

Nick found the pin with the knife's blade. He held the handle tight and lifted his feet off the floor to put all his weight into the task. The pin moved and the bolt popped.

With a chorus of squeals, the spider-heads dashed forward in a chaotic mob, the fast hopping over the slow. It sounded like a storm of hailstones sweeping toward them across the wooden plain.

Finch shoved the cage door with both hands. Nick was on the other side and the door slammed into him as it swung open, knocking him back and down. The little knife fell out of the lock and stuck upright, twanging, in the table's surface.

Finch snatched up the knife. He looked at Nick lying at his feet and paused for a moment. Then he saw the spider-heads closing in fast, and thought only of escape. He tucked the knife into the sheath at his calf, and reached through the bars of the cage for the bone with the thread wound around it. The other end of the thread was still knotted to Nick's cage. Finch ran backward to the edge of the table, holding the bone loosely so that it rolled in his hands and the thread unwound.

Nick got up, rubbing the back of his head, and turned in time to see Finch step back off the table's edge, just before the first of the spider-heads reached him.

"Thanks for the escape, Nick. You're on your own!" called Finch as he dropped out of sight. The thread snapped taut between him and the cage.

A small group of spider-heads broke ahead of the pack and swarmed upon Nick. He jumped and grabbed the bars of his cage, drawing his legs up beyond the reach of the clutching legs and stabbing fangs. He pulled himself up the bars and onto the solid roof of the cage and then turned, ready to kick the first ugly head that popped up.

The smooth, slender bars were an obstacle for the spider-heads. They tried to climb but lost their footing and slid back to the tabletop. For a moment Nick thought he'd found safe refuge from the monstrosities. But dozens more were arriving, and they crawled on top of their siblings and gripped the bars. The next to arrive climbed on top of those, and the heap of ugly heads and writhing legs piled up rapidly against the side of the cage. They would reach Nick in moments.

Finch looked something like a spider himself as he turned the bone in his hands and let the thread out slowly to lower himself from the table. When it was completely unwound, he would be close enough to drop to the floor without injury.

When Finch looked down, preparing to let go, he saw a group of spider-heads waiting for him, surrounding the spot where he would land. Above him, he saw three more beginning to follow him down the thread. Something splashed on Finch's cheek from above. It was a tiny drop of poison from one of those fangs. An instant after it landed, his cheek went cold and numb.

Finch swung his legs forward, then back, and started to swing. The spider-heads below scuttled back and forth to match his motion. Finch continued to thrust and kick, and the arc of his swing grew longer. The creatures below scrambled to keep up. Above him, the trio of spider-heads descended quickly.

Finch timed his release as best he could and flew out beyond the creatures. He laughed as he landed on his feet with athletic grace, while the abandoned thread and bone swung back and forth in the air. Only two spider-heads were on it now.

The pile of spider-heads had reached the top of Nick's cage. They spilled over the edge and ran at him. Nick hopped across to the other cage.

The spider-heads had not anticipated this, and none was waiting on top of the second cage to intercept the boy. He slid down the bars to the tabletop.

There was no way to follow Finch down the thread; the spider-heads blocked that path. Now the frantic horde was coming at him, spreading out to block every escape. Nick did the only thing left to do. He turned and sprinted to the end of the table, and when he reached the edge, he leaped out as far as his legs could propel him.

He was airborne forever, it seemed, running in space, and he thought for a moment that he would not make it over the wall surrounding the pool. The tip of his shoe even clipped the stone as he went by, and then he slapped the water hard. It stung every inch of him. He plunged deep into the cold black pool, and when he stopped sinking, he brought himself to the surface with a few hard kicks and a broad sweep of his arms.

Nick saw the spider-heads gathered along the edge of the table, wailing miserably. He shook his fist at the creatures and whooped in triumph. "Ha!"

* * *

Finch didn't see the smallest of the brood leap off the rope after him. Before he took his first step for the door, the leggy thing landed on his back and sprang for his neck, and he screamed and twisted as the tiny fangs pierced the skin behind his ear.

He reached over his shoulder and clawed at the spider-head. His fist closed around one of its legs and he whipped it over his head and dashed it to the floor. The skull broke in two against the stone, but the legs went on twitching and crawling, dragging the halves in opposite directions before their strength began to ebb.

Finch cursed, but the words came out in a mumble. The fangs had been in him for only an instant, but suddenly his neck and face were numb, and he couldn't feel his legs or arms anymore. He tried to lift his hand but it barely responded. Looking down, he saw his legs wobble, but it was like watching someone else's legs. He toppled over onto his back. He expected pain when his head struck the floor, but there was none—only the dull *thock* of head on stone.

The venom was selective. Finch could hear and see and breathe, but otherwise could barely move. He had fallen face up, staring at the ceiling. The other spider-heads were coming now. He could hear their little feet scrabbling across the floor. And then they were on him. He knew they were there, could vaguely sense them crawling over him. He tried to shake them off but could only manage a little twitch. One of the creatures climbed right onto his face and stared into his eyes for a moment before dipping its fangs into Finch's cheek.

Nick climbed out of the water and onto the wall at the edge of the pool. His stomach went sour as he saw Finch prone on the floor, with spider-heads all over him and more on the way. Then the door to Gnasher's room swung open, and the little creatures hopped off of Finch's body and ran for the shadows. Nick slipped back into the water. He let himself sink deep, then swam underwater to the other side of the pool where he would be out of sight behind the wall.

Gnasher was already in a foul mood from battling the flames, but his anger redoubled when he saw the open cages, the hanging thread, and Finch on the floor. Some of the spider-heads were slow to run away. Gnasher lifted his foot and squashed them flat. "Nettlesome bugs! Look what you've done to my captive!"

Gnasher scooped up Finch's limp body and stuffed him into the pouch he kept tied around his waist. Then he called out, in no particular direction, "Little morsel! Listen to me! I know you are here, hiding somewhere.

"I have no time to sniff you out, as much as I would like to. It is time to begin my conquest. But here is what I will do for you instead: Whenever I catch a child in the world below, I will tell them your name. Then I will crush them in the palm of my hand, in memory of Nick.

Your name will be the last thing they hear."

Gnasher cocked his head, listening, hoping perhaps that his words would cause Nick to cry out. Then he strode to the door. "Farewell then!" The door slammed shut behind him.

Nick climbed out of the water again and stood dripping on the wall. His chest was heaving, and his teeth and fists were clenched.

"It's not farewell. Not yet, you devil."

⊙ CHAPTER 19 ⊙

Nick dropped to the floor and raced for the door. The spider-heads gave him no trouble. Most were still on the edge of the table, weeping for him, or climbing back down the legs. The ones that ventured back from hiding gathered around their smashed brethren and lapped up the ooze. Nick kept a wary eye on them as he passed by, but they were intent on their meal. He was grateful to leave Gnasher's hellish room behind.

In the corridor, Nick took the knife from his pocket. It was a small weapon, but holding it made him feel a little braver.

Nick ran down the hallway. A thin haze collected at the ceiling high above. The closer he drew to the great hall, the thicker it became. The smell was pleasant compared to the castle's ambient reek.

He approached the great hall with care, in case Gnasher was lying in wait for him. But the ogre was not there. Although the fires in the hall were mostly out, heavy smoke from a second fire gushed from the opposite corridor.

There was no way to get to the treasure room now, but Nick did not care about the gold or jewels any more. He crossed the hall to the front door. Outside, it was liberating to see the open sky once again, and a steady breeze brought welcome fresh air. Nick breathed in, deep and long. Then he turned to the left and followed the wall around the perimeter of the castle.

He intended to put a slice in the rope—somehow.

Nick peered around the back corner. The cart was still there. Gnasher stood by it, looking around warily. Nick pulled his head back as the ogre glanced in his direction.

Nick wondered where Basher was, and then he heard the brutish ogre coughing violently. Risking another peek, he saw Basher emerge from the rear entrance, his arms heaped with weapons and armor. The brute ogre stumbled around, hacking and half-blind from the smoke inside the castle.

"Over here, fool!" Gnasher called impatiently. "Did you get all of it?"

Basher nodded. He brought the load to the cart and dumped it onto the flat area behind the spool. Then he leaned against the cart and tried to rub the sting out of his eyes with the back of his big fists.

"Come on, brother," said Gnasher. "We're leaving now."

"Uhh?" grunted Basher.

"We can't stay here with Mother lurking about trying

to ruin our plans, can we? Come on. We're getting out of this rotten place. Let the conquest begin." The ogres went to the front of the cart and took opposite sides of the crosspiece to push the cart along.

Nick slapped the wall in frustration. He had to get onto the cart now. Once it was moving, there would be no way to climb aboard. But it was a long run across open space to get there. He would certainly be seen.

Gnasher took a last look at the castle. He peered up at the roof, and his lip curled in a snarl. "Of all the times!" he said.

A white haze engulfed the castle and began to obscure the cart. At first Nick thought it was smoke from the raging fire. But no, this was wet and cool—another cloud was passing over the island, a gift from the heavens. Seconds later, the ogres disappeared in the fog.

"It will pass soon enough," he heard Gnasher mutter.

Nick did not know how long this good fortune would last. He sprinted for the cart. As he got closer, the shadowy figures of the ogres began to emerge. But the cloud provided adequate cover, and he slipped under the cart unseen.

Now that Nick was beneath the cart, he saw no easy way to climb aboard. The platform was far out of reach. He remembered that the giant wheels were as tall as the platform, and went to the rear wheel that was farthest from the ogres.

Nick found a large seam across the side of the wheel

and used it to pull himself up. He felt higher, along the curve of the wheel, but found no other place to hold on to.

The cloud was beginning to thin out as its tail end passed over the island. Nick could clearly see the legs of the ogres now at the front of the cart.

"Good-bye, Mother! Thanks for all the good work," Gnasher called back at the castle. Basher snickered. Together, they pushed on the crosspiece, muscles straining. The cart creaked and inched forward, slowly gaining momentum.

Nick saw only one desperate chance to get onto the cart. Before the seam in the wheel rose out of reach, he jumped and slid his fingers into the space. As the wheel turned, he was carried up. Soon he was at the top of the wheel, above the level of the platform. Praying that neither ogre would look back at that critical moment, Nick tucked his legs underneath him and sprang onto the platform. He scooted under the spool, out of sight.

The rope hung a few feet above the platform so the spool could rotate freely. Nick crawled into the narrow space like a crab. He looked at the knife in his hand. It was such a paltry tool for the task ahead of him: slicing through rope as thick and tough as a tree.

Nick got onto his knees and started cutting. The cart picked up speed as the ogres pulled it across the field, heading for the forest road. It bumped and jostled, making it hard to keep his balance.

Nick sawed furiously, but he was having little effect.

Only a few of the threads split open under his blade. He wished he had Finch's jagged knife with him. And he wondered what became of that man. Had the spider-heads poisoned him to death? Or was he now in the ogre's belly?

The gash was a fraction of an inch deep after several minutes, and Nick's arm ached from the effort. He looked at the knife. It was freshly sharpened when Nick found it, but now the edge was notched and blunted. Nick switched the knife to his left hand and went on cutting, pushing hard against the rope.

He looked out from under the spool and saw trees passing swiftly by. The cart rode over stones and stumps, shaking Nick's hand as he cut, and making it hard to keep the blade inside the groove he'd started. The dull knife slowed his progress further, but he thought that, with luck, he might slice deep enough by the time they arrived at the edge of the cloud island. His left hand was cramping, so he switched to his right again.

The cut was half an inch deep and Nick's hope began to grow—another inch or two might be enough to make the rope unravel—when one of the front wheels struck a large rock in the road. The cart lurched and came down hard. Nick bounced up into the rope and onto the platform again. The entire spool began to rotate above him, taking all the loops of rope with it. It did not stop until it made a full quarter-turn, and the little gash he had made was hopelessly out of reach.

Now there was no time to start a new cut, because the cart was emerging from the forest. In a few minutes they would reach the ridge at the edge of the cloud island.

With alarm, Nick realized how familiar the landscape looked. They were not far from where he'd first arrived, at the top of the beanstalk. Nick crawled to the front of the cart and peeked out. The massive backs of the ogres were in front of him. The brothers leaned forward, straining to pull the cart behind them. Basher seemed to have endless reserves of strength, but Gnasher was grunting and wheezing.

Up ahead the road disappeared into a cleft that the ogres had torn in the rocky ridge. The cart rumbled through the gap, into the sandy area beyond. Just a few hundred feet away, the low mists swirled over the coast.

There must be some way to stop them, Nick thought. He crawled into the machinery that would control the descent of the rope. He looked at the saw-toothed metal gears that meshed neatly together, searching for a way to foul up the contraption. But everything was so huge and solid, and all he had was the blunt little knife to work with.

The ogres struggled to pull the cart through the sand. Nick prayed that the wheels would become mired, stranding the rope just short of its destination, but the ogres heaved mightily, and the cart kept moving through the sand and into the mists with hard ground underneath.

"So close," Gnasher panted. "Almost there!"

It seemed inevitable now: Gnasher and Basher would reach the world below. There was nothing Nick could do but climb down the beanstalk and try to warn whoever would listen about the horror that was coming. At least he could return to Jack's fortress and give the old man Gullinda's message.

But getting off the cart was a challenge that Nick had not considered. The platform towered high above the ground. Below him the mist hovered a few feet over the rocks. As breezes whipped along the edge of the cloud island, they made the vapors swirl. Part of the ground would be revealed for a moment, and it was treacherous, full of cracks and craters and sharp jutting stones. He was likely to break his leg if he jumped.

"Stop! Close enough! We're here!" Gnasher yelled. The cart rolled to a halt. Gnasher and his brother lay down to catch their breath.

"At last," Gnasher said, panting. "All that planning. All that work. Now we're going to do what our father tried to do and failed. We're going to their world. Go on, Basher, secure the cart like I taught you."

Basher got up obediently. When Nick realized what the ogre was doing, he saw his chance to get off the cart.

There were four chains heaped on the platform, each secured to a corner. At the other end of the chains were long metal spikes. Basher took the first chain and stepped back from the cart until it was fully extended. Then he used a hammer to drive the spike deep into the ground. As soon as the first chain was secured, he started on the second.

It would be easy for Nick to climb down one of the chains. The trick was to make sure he wouldn't be seen. He looked out into the sky, hoping to see a cloud coming this way that might provide the safe cover of fog, but the horizon was clear. He'd have to wait until the ogres' backs were turned and take his chances. If he reached the ground, he could stay low, and the mist might keep him out of sight.

Nick was shocked to see just how close the ogres had come to the peninsula where the beanstalk grew. It was hardly a hundred yards away. Nick could see the great boulder where the plant had attached itself, and even a few tendrils that wrapped around it. If the ogres looked in that direction, they would be certain to notice it.

While Basher drove in the spikes, Gnasher sat on the ground, still breathless. "You remember how it works, don't you? I've told you enough times," he said. "I get in the harness and go down first with the weapons. The weight of the rope is enough to make the spool turn, and the little wheels and gears control the speed of the descent. Now, while I'm being lowered, don't touch anything. When the rope is completely let out, you reel it back in. Then all you have to do is get in the harness and drop yourself over the edge. Can you remember that?"

Basher grunted something that sounded like yes.

"Now," said Gnasher, "how about a little treat before

the trip, brother?" Nick watched as Gnasher reached into the pouch at his waist and pulled out the limp body of Finch. Basher came lumbering over, licking his lips, to get a closer look.

Still alive? Nick wondered. He was sure he didn't want to see what was about to happen.

Gnasher held Finch by the foot and let him dangle upside down. "An army of these won't give us much trouble, will they, Basher?"

Finch began to moan softly.

"Well, our little friend is waking up," said Gnasher. He gave Finch a shake. "Let's see what he has to say for himself now." Gnasher flipped Finch over into his other hand and waited for him to fully awaken.

Finch barely resembled the arrogant, handsome leader of thieves that Nick had known. His ruddy complexion was drained of color, except for the trickling red holes that the spider-heads left behind. His lips were pulled back, and his teeth were clenched together in a mad grin. There was a strange, dazed look in his eyes; perhaps the venom was still affecting his brain.

Finch's head swiveled back and forth as he stared with dread at the gruesome monsters before him.

"Yes, wake up—it is time to accept your punishment," Gnasher said. "You should not have tried to escape. You've made me enormously angry."

"It was the boy's idea! Not mine!" Finch's words were slurred, and there was lunacy in his voice.

"Little liar," said Gnasher. He reached out and pinched Finch's head between his thumb and forefinger. He began to squeeze.

"No!" screamed Finch. He threw his arms around the fingers in a futile attempt to pry them apart. "The boy is the liar! He lied to you! I can help you! I can lead you to Jack—the man who killed your father!"

"What's that you say?" Gnasher said. His eyebrows went up and his nose twitched. He released Finch's head, and Basher began to bounce in place as he squatted.

Finch's words chilled Nick to the core. The man would say anything now to save himself.

While the ogres were distracted, Nick saw his opportunity to climb down unnoticed. As he crawled on hands and knees to the back of the cart, he could still hear the conversation between Gnasher and Finch.

"Tell me about this Jack—and how you can help us," Gnasher said.

"Yes! I can help! Let me guide you. I'll show you where Jack lives, the one who stole from your father. And that's not all—I'll lead you to other places. I know other castles, full of treasures! And villages full of people—thousands of fat, juicy people! Just let me live, and I'll be your guide!"

Nick clambered down the chain, as fast as he dared. When he was near the end he dropped to the ground, knee-deep in mist. He was halfway between panic and rage from listening to Finch, who would betray an entire world to preserve his own life. Moving as quickly as he could through the mist, and trying not to stumble over hidden stones, Nick headed for the beanstalk. The ogres' backs were still turned to him.

"Where will we find Jack?" Gnasher said.

"Old Man Jack! Living like a king on your father's gold! In a fortress, a white fortress, not far from the beanstalk. I'll take you there!"

"But the beanstalk has been destroyed."

"No! Another of the boy's lies! I told you, I'm the one you can trust!"

"The beanstalk is still here?" Gnasher said. He slapped his forehead with the heel of his hand. "Of course it's still here. Basher, I've been a fool!"

Gnasher lifted Finch to his face. "Tell me where it is. Now."

"Oh, no," Nick whispered to himself. He glanced back. Now that Gnasher had raised Finch high, Nick could see the man over the ogre's shoulder. Finch was looking for the beanstalk and spotted him on the ground below.

Nick shook his head and put a finger to his lips, begging Finch not to betray his presence. Time seemed to hesitate for a long, silent moment. Then Finch's hand came up and he pointed at Nick.

"There he is!" shrieked Finch. "The boy! Running to the beanstalk! He's the one you want! Kill him and let me help you conquer the world below!"

"As if we need your help!" snapped Gnasher. "You've already told us how to find Jack." He stuffed the kicking and hollering Finch back into the pouch at his waist. "Let's get that one, Basher!" Basher rose up and thundered toward Nick. Gnasher ran to the cart and reached into the pile of weapons.

Nick gave up caution and ran. He had a head start, but he did not think it was enough.

Finch had always been the hunter, not the prey. Now he was helpless in the clutches of something as evil-hearted as he was, but far more powerful—a monster that could snap every bone in his body with a squeeze of his fist.

In the darkness of the sack, he moaned as he was bounced against the ogre's thigh. His head rang from the squeeze that Gnasher's fingers had given it, and his thoughts spun out of control. What a terrible sensation, for his skull to feel so fragile in that monstrous pinch. The ogre could have cracked his head as easily, and with as little remorse, as Finch cracked a nut. *And probably for the same reason,* a voice in his head called out. *Because he wants the meat inside!* Finch began to laugh again, an eerie giggle he could not contain.

His thoughts twisted and spun. It was as if a mob was inside his head, shouting one another down. The worst of it was a part of him was still sane, and it knew he was slipping into madness.

Get the knife, the one sane voice urged him.

"I lost the knife!" Finch moaned.

The other knife, it whispered. And Finch remembered the smaller blade strapped to his ankle. He reached down and pulled it from the sheath. He stabbed at the bottom of the pouch, and the blade pierced the thick material, all the way to the haft. Finch grabbed the handle with both hands and began to pull the blade toward him. He sawed up and down with manic strength, cutting a slit for his escape.

As Basher ran past the cart in pursuit of Nick, his foot caught the chain that secured the cart and he tumbled onto the ground.

"Idiot!" yelled Gnasher. "Stay down and watch." Nick risked a look back, expecting the ogres to be on top of him already. Instead he saw Gnasher raise a familiar-looking weapon. It was the crossbow; Nick had seen its design on the paper he retrieved from Gnasher's room.

The ogre pulled the trigger, and a hundred arrows whistled through the air. Nick dropped to the ground and curled up, making himself as small as he could. An instant later he heard the arrows clattering all around. One bounced off the ground and fell harmlessly across his legs. Nick sprang up and ran for the beanstalk again.

Gnasher snarled in disgust and dropped the crossbow. He ran after Nick, and Basher got to his feet again and followed.

Nick heard heavy feet pounding the ground behind

him. The impacts grew more intense as the ogres closed the distance. Nick turned for a glimpse. The ogres filled the sky behind him, Gnasher in front and Basher a few strides behind. When their feet came down, little stones bounced off the ground and up out of the mists.

"We're right behind you, morsel!" yelled Gnasher.

Nick turned onto the narrow neck of land that led to the beanstalk. The huge boulder and the top of the beanstalk were just ahead. Nick's legs were wobbly from the long hard dash. Out of the corner of his eye, he saw one of Gnasher's feet come down right beside him. He couldn't see the grasping hand with the long, pointy fingers coming toward him, but he knew it was there nevertheless. He heard Gnasher scream: *Got you now!*

Suddenly Nick's feet weren't finding solid ground anymore. Too late, he remembered the gaping hole that he'd discovered when he first arrived on the cloud island. He screamed.

One moment, Nick was falling through the foggy shaft, expecting to smash into a rocky bottom. The next, he burst through the mist into the clear air below, and he saw the world far beneath him.

Then the beanstalk was coming at him in a rush. Nick was running directly at it when he fell through the hole; now his momentum carried him the rest of the way. He put his hands and feet out to brace himself, turned his face to the side, and slammed into the dense mass of tendrils and leaves at a crushing speed.

Nick nearly bounced off and out into space again, but he seized a branch with one hand. The force of the impact left him woozy. His hands and arms were exhausted from trying to cut through the rope, and his lungs were on fire from the run. He began to slip.

Then he felt that strange tingling sensation again—the infectious life force of the beanstalk. It surged through the muscles of his arms and legs, and he gripped the branches with renewed strength.

Gnasher saw the boy suddenly drop from sight into the mist. He took two short steps to keep himself from following the boy down and felt his toes dangling over the edge of a hole. Basher, following close behind, did not anticipate his brother's sudden stop, and ran into Gnasher's back. Gnasher shouted, his arms flailed, and he toppled into the gap. Basher reached out and grabbed his brother's legs before he slipped all the way through.

Clinging to the beanstalk, Nick looked up to see Gnasher emerge headfirst through the hole, dropping all the way to his waist. Then a startling thing occurred.

There was a pouch dangling at Gnasher's side. A figure, with a knife in hand, popped feet-first through a slit in the bottom. It was Finch. He fell right past Nick, nearly close enough to touch. For the last time, their eyes met. Nick saw Finch's expression change in an instant, from the joy of sudden freedom to a cold realization of inescapable death.

Finch opened his mouth as if to speak. But if he said anything, the wind carried the words away. Nick could do nothing but watch him go, shrinking away to a tiny black figure before vanishing altogether.

Nick looked over at Gnasher. The ogre was gaping at the world beneath him, a legendary world he had heard of but never seen.

"Wait—don't pull me up yet! I see it, brother! The world of little people! It's right there!" Gnasher let out a blood-chilling, jubilant howl.

Nick swung around to the other side of the beanstalk. If he could hide before Gnasher noticed him, the ogre might think he, too, had fallen to his doom.

"Oh, don't think I didn't see you, Nick!" Gnasher said. "I lost your unlucky friend, but we'll catch up with you soon enough. You're first on the menu. And then we're going to see a little old man named Jack. Perhaps he's a friend of yours. I've heard he lives not far from here!"

Nick leaned out to face the ogre. "If you come down, you'll both end up as dead as your father!"

"We'll see about that, morsel! Go on, hurry down the beanstalk! We'll be with you shortly," Gnasher jeered. He called to his brother. "What are you waiting for, idiot? Pull me up!"

Nick watched Gnasher rise. The ogre looked at him with his red-pink eyes flashing and a sinister grin on his face, waving with his fingers as he rose into the hole and disappeared from view.

* * *

Basher pulled his brother out of the gap and onto solid ground. He let Gnasher's feet go and began to hop around excitedly, slapping at the ground. He ran around the hole to the tip of the peninsula and gestured at the beanstalk that rose out of the fog.

"Yes, I see it. Don't follow him yet, Basher," called Gnasher. "You can climb down soon enough. We must put on armor first and bring some weapons. The morsel may have friends down there. Just wait until they see us coming—what a day this will be for Gnasher and Basher!"

The two ogres loped back to the cart to prepare for their assault.

I'm free! was the first thing Finch thought as he slipped through the slit in the sack. *I'm dead* was the second. As Finch began to fall, he saw the traitor Nick clinging to the beanstalk. Finch tried to say "Help me," but he couldn't get the words out fast enough, and then the boy was gone.

The beanstalk was tantalizingly near. He reached for it, tried to swim through the air for it, but could not get close enough for even his fingertips to brush the leaves. Then the breeze caused him to drift away from the plant, and grabbing it was beyond hope. The wind whistled and roared, snapping through his garments and tearing the little knife out of his hand. The knife fell alongside him, doing a strange dance in the air as the wind turned it this way and that. Finch began to tumble. He saw the earth below him, the cloud island above, the earth below, the cloud island above. With each revolution, the earth rose closer and the cloud island flew higher.

It was near the end of day now, and the sun was dropping below the far edge of the cloud, which stretched nearly to the western horizon. The light made everything look like gold.

Gold, gold, gold . . .

Suddenly, mercifully, the last lone voice of sanity flickered and died, and the leader of the band of thieves laughed heartily the rest of the way down.

The instant Gnasher was out of sight, Nick began frantically to climb down the beanstalk. He thought that any second now the plant would begin to shake and he would know that one or both of the ogres was coming after him. And they would close in fast— because unlike Jack's giant, there was no broken foot to slow them.

Nick descended in a rush, taking one reckless chance after another. When he came to a coiling tendril, he seized the tip of it with both hands and leaped out into the air, and the coil unwound and dropped him a dozen yards, springing him up and down when fully extended, and then he dropped onto the branch below to climb down some more. When he spotted a broad leaf directly underneath he simply plopped onto it in a seated position, and the leaf would tilt and he would slide to the branch or the tendril below. He didn't look down at the earth or up at the cloud island. All his concentration was on the beanstalk, searching for the next handhold, the next foothold, the next limb or leaf or tendril. To think of anything else for an instant would surely lead to a fatal mistake. As he jumped and clambered and swung and sprang, he chanted aloud, "Got to get down, got to get down, got to get down . . ."

There was a sudden gust of wind, and it moved a leaf that he was about to grab. Nick fell, and the branch below struck him in the thighs. He spun head over heels, out of control. As he tumbled he saw a tendril below and he tried to seize the end as he went by. It slipped through his hands, but not before he slowed himself and controlled his spin. He fell like a cat, arms and feet pointing down, and the plunge ended abruptly as a broad horizontal branch slammed into his gut. Nick let loose a loud "Oof!" He crawled along the branch to the main trunk of the beanstalk and rested for a moment to let the pain subside. Nothing seemed to be broken.

Nick was elated to see that he was well beyond the halfway point in his climb. He leaned back and looked up, but there was no sign of either ogre overhead. And the beanstalk was not trembling, as Nick supposed it would under their heavy hands and feet. All that he felt was the pulse of churning, pumping water from deep inside the trunk.

He didn't know what was taking them so long to pursue him, but he was grateful for it. Perhaps he could reach the bottom before the ogres after all—early enough, even, to do something about them.

Now the sun had dropped below the cloud island and would soon set behind the western horizon. For a moment Nick marveled over everything that happened to him in the course of a single day. Then, knowing that he had to act quickly if he wanted to see another sunrise, he resumed his descent.

CHAPTER 20

The band of thieves was uneasy, after keeping watch at the foot of the beanstalk all day. That morning, after the beanstalk sprouted, Finch had found them cowering in the forest and demanded that they return. Nobody wished to, but Finch and his jagged knife could be utterly convincing.

So they came back and watched Finch climb the beanstalk on a quest for treasure and revenge. "I'll be back with the boy's blood on my knife and the giant's gold in my sack," he told them. "You all stay here and keep the curious away. I don't want anybody chopping this beastie down while I'm up there. Toothless, you make sure nobody gets any other ideas."

"Aye," said Toothless John. The thug had packed cool mud on his face and arms to soothe the pain of the hundred stings he'd suffered when the wasps were driven mad by the erupting beanstalk.

Finch had climbed up a little way, then turned to call once more.

"So, Squint, the story was true after all. That really *was* the Jack who climbed the beanstalk. Who'd have believed it?" Squint just stared back at him, wondering if he would see his leader again, and half hoping that he wouldn't.

Now the whole day had passed with no sign of Finch. The gang had waited for its leader before, but this was different in so many strange ways. There was the awesome plant, with its slithering roots, strange sounds coming from within, and the weird tingling one felt when he drew close. There was that cloud overhead, an oppressive mass that made the air feel thick and heavy, and cast a shadow across the land until just a few minutes ago when the sun finally sunk back into view above the western horizon. And finally there was the feeling that many in the band shared—that someone was watching them.

If it had not been for Toothless John, eyeing them all and wandering over to eavesdrop when the others would whisper among themselves, many of them would have deserted, even at the risk of incurring Finch's wrath.

Toothless John glared as he saw Pewt standing by the campfire, muttering something to Squint and Marlowe. The trio came over to where Toothless John was sitting, applying fresh mud to his puffy wounds.

"Listen, Toothless," said Pewt. "Just how long do we have to stay here? We've had all we can take of this place."

Toothless stood and cracked his knuckles, towering a full head over the burly Pewt. But before either could speak, they heard something from the air above, like howling laughter. At first it was a distant sound, and then it was right on top of them, and there came a splintering crash in a tree nearby. Branches snapped and leaves fluttered in all directions.

And the body of a man was lodged in the remaining branches, twisted and broken.

Toothless let out a moan and ran to the body. He lifted the head to look into the face and screamed. Weeping, he fell to his knees. The rest of the gang looked on nervously. Pewt and Marlowe nodded to each other, and slunk toward the woods. A few of the others started to creep off as well.

Toothless looked up and saw them leaving. "Traitors! Get back here! All of you!"

No one answered him. Instead they broke into a dash, across the dry streambed and into the trees. Only Squint was left, and even he was beginning to back away. Toothless pulled his knife out and raised it over his shoulder, holding it by the blade, poised to throw. "Not another step, Squint—unless you can run with a knife in your back." He pointed up the beanstalk. "That boy, that runt must have done this. You stay right here and tell me when you see him coming."

Squint sat on the ground looking up at the beanstalk. He puffed his cheeks and let the air whistle slowly out between his lips. "I hope that boy is all that's coming down."

When Nick was only a few hundred feet off the ground, he slowed to a less frenzied pace. No sense falling to his death now, so close to earth.

He thought he felt a slight tremble coming down through the beanstalk. Or maybe he was just imagining it.

But there it was again.

Below him was the forsaken farm. The details began to resolve themselves as he came down—the little house with the roof partly caved in, the stone well with the beanstalk roots filling the shaft and rupturing the walls. There, too, were the stump and the ax. It was the ax that Nick wanted most of all right now.

He saw a breeze sweep across the fields below. Clouds of dust swirled in the wind. It looked as if the valley was in the throes of a seven-year drought.

Nick felt a stronger tremor in the beanstalk, and there was no doubt now: At least one of the ogres was coming. He finished the climb and dropped to the ground, glad to feel the sturdy earth under his feet. He ran toward the ax in the stump. His eyes stung a little from the dust, and from the smoke of the smoldering campfire.

Campfire? Nick wondered who had been camped out at the farmhouse when something hit him from behind. He crumpled onto the parched dirt, raising a cloud of dust. Toothless John stood overhead, with a club in one hand and a knife in the other, and Squint stood behind him.

Toothless looked like a wild man. His shirt was off, and his whole body was caked with mud. Where the mud had cracked and fallen, Nick saw whitish welts. The skin around Toothless's eyes was puffed, and his eyes were nearly shut.

Toothless lifted his boot and brought it down on Nick's neck. "See what you've done? Care to explain what happened to Finch?" With his foot, Toothless pushed Nick's head to one side, and he saw Finch's dead form tangled in the tree's branches.

"Cut it down!" Nick could barely choke the words out. "We have to cut the beanstalk down!"

Toothless John scowled. The boot pressed harder. "Don't try to scare me, you little pup. I'll teach you to—"

Something large and green fell with a plop next to Nick's head. It was a torn leaf from the beanstalk. Then a rustling noise caught Toothless John's attention. The beanstalk was beginning to shake. From high above, a roaring sound came rolling down. It was like the first distant thunder of a storm.

"What's *that?*" asked Squint. He craned his neck upward.

Nick knew. "Still time! Chop it down!" he croaked.

Nothing could be seen yet. But the sound was growing. Up there something was howling with anger. Now every leaf on the beanstalk was trembling. Another broken leaf fluttered down from on high.

"Squint?" said Toothless, keeping his foot pressed against Nick's neck. "You see anything?" Squint shielded his eyes with a trembling hand and looked up. For a moment he just stood there. Then he let out a gasp. With his eyes bulging, Squint simply turned and ran, kicking up dust behind him. Only Toothless was left. He looked down at Nick, back up the beanstalk, and over at Finch's body in the tree.

"Please, John," pleaded Nick in a rasping voice. "Help me cut it down. Before he gets here—before *both* of them get here. So many people will die if we don't stop them. We're the only ones who can do this."

Toothless John took his foot away and stepped back. "I . . . I can't," he stammered. And he ran off.

"No!" cried Nick. "You've got to help me!" He got up, clutching his bruised and aching throat, and ran to the ax. He pulled furiously on the handle, but it slipped out of his hand, filling his palms with splinters, and he fell into the dust again. The beanstalk was rocking harder now. More pieces rained onto the ground. Now Nick could see an ogre, still high above, but coming fast, bellowing horribly.

Nick ran back to the stump and gripped the handle anew. The splinters drove deeper into his palms, but he ignored the stinging. He jerked on the ax handle again, and it wouldn't budge. Three more times he yanked, grunting loudly. Did it move a little on the last try? He wasn't sure, but he grabbed the handle again, put his legs on the stump beside the buried blade, and with all the power he could muster, he pulled and screamed, "*Come . . . on . . . OUT!*" and it did come out, and he flew backward with the ax handle in his hands, rolling as he hit the dusty ground.

With a triumphant shout, Nick picked up the ax handle—and realized with a shock that all he had was the handle. It had separated from the head of the ax. The blade was still buried in the stump.

There was the ogre, just a few hundred feet from the ground. In minutes he would be down. And Basher knew it. He paused to celebrate with a roar.

Nick threw the useless handle away. It raised another cloud of dust in the dry dead ground.

The dry dead ground. The dry dead grass. The fire, thought Nick.

Racing to the campfire the thugs had built, he grabbed the unburned end of a flaming log and lobbed it at the base of the beanstalk. The grass ignited in an instant. But it would burn out quickly. Nick looked around for more fuel.

Dead bushes were all around. With their roots shriveled and the soil sucked dry by the monstrous thirst of the beanstalk, they pulled out easily, and Nick tossed three into the fire. They burst into flame.

"Smart lad!" called a voice from far away. Nick turned

and saw Old Man Jack and three of his men coming down the hillside in a horse-drawn wagon. The slope was steep and the wagon hurtled along at a perilous speed. The four passengers were nearly bounced out. One of the younger men had a grip on Jack's shoulder for safekeeping.

The cart was out of control. It hit one stone hard and tilted dangerously, riding on only two wheels for a perilous moment before slamming down on all four again. By some miracle they reached the bottom of the hill without either horse breaking a leg.

Now that they were close, Nick recognized two of Jack's men: One was Roland, the guard from the gallery, the other was Henry, the driver in the forest.

"Roland! Henry! Bill! Help feed the flames," called Jack.

With the loudest roar yet, Basher resumed his climb down. The horses reared up in fright, and the wagon lurched backward, sending Jack's men tumbling to the ground as they tried to get off. Unhurt, they leaped to their feet, and began heaving everything they could find onto the growing fire: a dozen more bushes, the fence posts from the pasture, the broken rain barrel, boards from the ramshackle farmhouse.

Now the flames leaped twenty feet high, and the fire spread into the brush all around the trunk. As the men kept fueling the flames, Nick stood back to watch. Then an ear-shattering roar exploded in the air just over their heads.

Basher is here. He stopped just above the fire, not thirty feet from the ground, and hissed at the little people below.

Basher wore the lightweight armor that was woven from the beanstalk plants, and a studded metal helmet on his head. Across his back he wore that awful scythe with a blade so long it could slice through an army with one broad sweep. But Basher's first enemy in the world below was a roaring fire.

The flames licked at his feet, and he howled. The smoke stung his eyes, and he closed them. The smoke filled his lungs, and he choked and spat. He moved a little up the beanstalk. The blaze went higher, and he climbed some more. The fire spread in an ever-widening circle, driving everyone back.

The flames seared the foot of the beanstalk, and the skin of the intertwined stalks blistered as the waters inside began to boil. The roots pulled out of the ground, writhing and twisting as if in pain.

Shudders reverberated up the mighty plant. Just above the flames, the leaves began to curl and wither, and the entire beanstalk crisped and burned at the bottom. Steam hissed out of tiny fissures all around it. The stalks began to swell outward in all directions, as a fierce pressure built from inside.

"Turn away!" called Jack as the first bulge erupted, triggering a cluster of explosions. Painfully hot, gleaming green waters shot everywhere. Nick spun around and pulled the cowl over his head, but the scorching droplets stung the skin on his back as they soaked through his clothes. When the waters stopped raining down, he pulled back the cowl and turned around to look.

"Good heavens," whispered Jack.

The beanstalk had blown itself apart at the trunk. It hung in the air, swaying back and forth like a slow pendulum. The ogre dangled just above the fire, hugging the severed beanstalk and bellowing as the flames scorched his legs.

Then the beanstalk suddenly dropped like a spike, driving deep into the loose dusty earth, and a plume of dust and smoke billowed up. The fire dwindled, choked by the dust.

When the breeze cleared the dust away, Nick saw Basher buried to his knees in the ground, struggling to free himself, blinded by the smoke. The ogre raised one thick leg out of the dust. As he fought to free the other, the beanstalk began to fall limp all around him in gigantic loops. It started slowly and picked up speed, laying overlapping coils. Basher drew out the other leg, freeing himself entirely, but a length of the beanstalk fell across his shoulders, driving him to his knees.

"It's coming down—the whole thing's coming down! Get away!" Nick shouted, grabbing Jack by the sleeve.

He and the others ran toward the hillside to escape the falling coils. From a safer distance, they turned to watch. There was a high whistling in the heavens. Far above, Nick saw the top of the beanstalk outracing the rest as it plunged earthward with a giant arc of green behind it. At the tip of the falling plant, Nick saw something large and gray, gathering speed, and shrieking ominously as it tore through the air.

Nick recognized the great boulder on which the beanstalk had been anchored. The weight of the severed beanstalk had wrenched it from its perch at the island's edge. With the tendrils still around it, it looked as if a great hand was bringing the stone down to smite the monster. Basher saw it coming and threw his hands up as if he could ward it off.

When the boulder landed, it was moving almost too fast for Nick to see. First Basher was there, wild-eyed and howling and smoldering from the fire. Then he was gone, and another, far greater cloud of dust and rock shot into the sky. Jack's hand clamped onto his shoulder and pulled him to the ground. Nick clasped his hands behind his head as the dust cloud engulfed the group. Rocks pelted all around him, some of them dangerously large. From nearby, he heard a grunt of pain.

For a minute afterward he could hear the remains of the beanstalk falling to the earth. Then finally everything was quiet. Nick rolled onto his back. The air was still clogged with dust, but the gentle breeze from the east was beginning to clear it, and he could breathe and see a little.

Where Basher stood, only a shallow crater was left.

Even the great boulder was gone, driven deep into the ground. Pieces of the beanstalk were looped everywhere, half covered with dirt and soil. The roots that had pulled themselves out of the earth twitched pitifully, like the legs of a crushed insect, the last traces of life ebbing away.

The fire had been snuffed out by the dust and the impact. In the stream nearby, the waters began to flow again, no longer intercepted by the wormy roots of the dead beanstalk. They gurgled over the mud in the streambed, filling the cracks, and soon the stream was reborn.

Nick heard Jack's men coughing. They were getting to their feet, brushing off the inch of fine dirt that coated everything. Henry was looking about urgently. He waved at the dust, trying to clear it. "Master Jack?" he called out.

Nick knew the old man had been right beside him. He looked over and saw Jack on the ground, unmoving, with his face in the ground. A fist-sized rock was on the ground beside him. Blood was soaking through the dust on the back of his head.

"Jack!" screamed Nick. He crawled over to the inert body. "Are you all right?"

Jack's men were there in a second. Henry gently rolled the old man over. "Master Jack, can you hear me? Talk to me, Jack. Please, sir, open your eyes!" Bill and Roland looked at each other, heartsick.

Nick put his mouth close to Jack's ear. "Jack, you can't

leave me now. I came back with a message. Gullinda asked me to tell you something. You have to hear it!"

Jack's eyebrows twitched. A little smile came to the old man's face. The eyelids fluttered open, and he looked over at Nick. He coughed a little, and started to say something, but suddenly the smile vanished and his eyes focused on a distant point.

"A . . . a . . . another one!" he said hoarsely. Nick looked around. Henry gasped, and Roland swore.

To the west, Gnasher was dropping out of the sky. Like his brother, he was helmeted and dressed in the green-brown woven armor. A sword and knife hung from his belt. He stood on a mesh sack that was suspended underneath the rope and bristled with pointy weapons.

The rope came down in increments, dropping a foot at a time and pausing with clockwork regularity. Nick could picture the spool turning slowly on the cart high above and the saw-toothed gears of the machine controlling the descent.

Gnasher would soon touch down near the bottom of the hillside, not a hundred yards from the smoldering remains of the beanstalk and the little group of people. From his airborne perch, strapped tightly into a harness that was secured to the rope, he had seen his brother's spectacular death. He shook his fist at the people below and screamed from on high.

"I saw what you did! Oh, you will suffer! Starting with you, morsel!" Then Gnasher let loose an unearthly cry, something between a hiss and a howl, that echoed against the hillside. Jack's horses pawed at the air in fright.

Jack sat up. He put a hand to the bloody patch on the back of his head. "Bill. Roland. Get me one of your longbows, then get out of here. Take Henry and the boy with you."

"We're *all* getting out of here," corrected Roland. He helped the old man up. "Master Jack, we can't take that monster on, just the four of us. We'll be lucky just to outrun him."

"Listen—this is my lot, Roland," Jack said in a steely voice. "I nearly caused disaster the last time I let a beanstalk grow. I've done it for real this time. Somehow, this is all my fault. This thing is here now because I went up to that cloud so many years ago. Isn't it, Nick?"

Nick did not want to say yes, and he did not want to lie. He turned away.

"You see? It *is* true," said Jack. "It is my fault alone, so I'm staying here to fight alone. And if I die, all the better. I cannot live knowing that this beast was unleashed because of my foolishness."

"We won't let you do it," said Bill.

"I've killed a giant before!" yelled Jack.

"No, you haven't," said Nick, but nobody paid attention.

Gnasher took a knife and cut the mesh sack loose from the rope. It crashed to the ground below him and rolled a little down the slope. As he dropped the last few feet, he turned to call to the little group. "How kind of you to wait for me! I'm famished after such a long journey!" The ogre stretched his legs and touched the ground with his toes. The rope began to coil on the ground behind him, still ratcheting down. "Gnasher is here, world of men! Gnasher the clever! Gnasher the conqueror!"

"Come on!" Roland gave Nick and Jack a shove toward the wagon. Nick climbed on, but Jack snatched up a bow and a quiver full of arrows and ran as fast as his old legs could carry him toward Gnasher. Roland cursed and ran after him. "Come back here, Jack! You'll get all of us killed!"

"Did you say *Jack*? Yes, come to me, Jack! I was planning to visit you—and here you are to welcome me!" Gnasher laughed. He'd begun to unfasten the first of five buckles that secured him in the harness, but paused to draw his sword.

Roland and Bill caught up to Jack and wrapped their arms around the old man. Jack tried to wriggle free, but his men were stronger by far, and they dragged Jack back toward the wagon. Gnasher grinned, putting the sword on the ground and returning to the buckles. And that was when Nick saw something happening behind the ogre.

The rope had begun to uncoil and slide up the hill. *But why*, Nick wondered, and the breeze at his back reminded him. *The beanstalk isn't there anymore—the cloud island can move again!*

"Jack's right," he shouted to Henry. "We have to attack!" He climbed into the back of the wagon and pulled out a pair of spears.

"Have you lost your wits as well?" said Henry.

"We just have to distract him for a moment—look at the rope!" Nick hopped down, handed one spear to Henry, and ran at the ogre. Henry understood at last and followed. Jack and Roland and Bill were so startled to see them go by, holding their spears high and screaming, that they forgot their struggle.

"We're coming to kill you, Gnasher!" Nick shouted.

"Are we the only ones who don't want to die?" Bill asked Roland.

Gnasher had unfastened the second buckle, and he looked up when he heard Nick's voice. His grin grew wider. "Oh, this is even better. Yes, come to me, little Nick. You and your friend, come to me."

The ogre bent to pick up his sword, but the rope tugged at him from behind, and the weapon was somehow out of reach. "What?" he muttered, and then he was pulled over onto his back. The rope began to drag him, slowly but irresistibly, up the slope.

High above, on the cloud island, she found the machine that lowered the infernal rope. She watched it for a while as the line fed out a yard at a time, the teeth of the gears clicking mechanically away. There was still plenty left on the spool.

Reaching into the mist, she felt about and found a loose rock of considerable size. She crammed it into the place where the gears meshed. The teeth bit into the rock, trying to shatter it. But the rock resisted, and the machine ground to a halt. She hoped she had not arrived too late.

The giantess looked at her shadow and waited for it to dance.

Nick saw the narrow band of sky at the horizon begin to widen and remembered how the cloud island had descended to meet the growing beanstalk. So now it was rising back to its normal height, taking the rope *up* as well as away, and pulling the ogre with it.

Gnasher screamed and scratched and clawed at the slope below him. He rolled onto his back and fumbled at the three remaining buckles of the harness. The rope was gathering speed. His helmet popped off and clattered down the hillside, past Nick and the men.

The ogre was approaching the top of the hill rapidly. He saw it coming and gave up on the buckles. Pulling out his knife, he hacked at the straps of the harness. He sliced through one quickly. He was halfway through the remaining one when he reached the crest of the hill.

Gnasher gave a shrill cry as he soared out into space and the ground dropped away beneath him. The second strap began to weaken, and he grabbed the rope above just before it snapped.

If Gnasher had let go in that instant, when he was not far above the ground, Nick thought he might have been able to land without serious injury. But he did not. The ogre hesitated, gaping down at the world he'd come to conquer. Then he was hundreds of feet aloft, and the opportunity was gone.

Nick and Jack and Roland and Henry and Bill stood together and watched without speaking as the ogre was carried away, clinging to the rope and rising higher and higher. The cloud island flew out to the west, toward the open sea. At last the sun emerged above the retreating cloud island, and the shadows that had fallen across the land disappeared in a burst of golden radiance.

Finally Henry turned to Nick.

"Are there any more of those . . . things?"

"No, I guess that's all of them," said Nick.

"How long do you suppose he can hang on to that rope?" asked Bill.

"I don't know," said Nick.

"Think he can climb back up?" asked Roland.

"It's an awful long way," said Nick.

Jack kneeled beside him.

"How's your head, sir?" asked Nick.

"I'll be fine. Those two, Nick . . . were they who I think they were?"

"Yes, sir. The sons of the giant. *Her* sons, too."

A thrill of hope ran through the old man's bones. "Her sons! So she didn't die that day!"

"No, sir. And she's still alive. Gullinda gave me a message for you. There are some things you ought to know."

Jack put his hands on Nick's shoulders. "Tell me what she told you. Please."

Nick looked over at the others. "I'd kind of like to say it in private. I guess it's personal."

Henry and Roland and Bill had been watching. They shrugged and smiled and went to the wagon.

"Whisper," said Jack. He turned his head to one side so Nick could speak quietly into his ear.

Nick closed his eyes and whispered. He told Jack about the story the giantess told him. About the love she still had for Jack, despite everything he had done. Nick talked about what really happened the day the giant died. About the peace that Gullinda found, however brief, after that day. Nick told Jack about the new suffering that she endured. About how her suffering was over now, perhaps forever, because of what happened after Jack gave Nick the beans. And he gave Jack the message that the giantess had asked him to remember.

"I have not forgotten, but I have forgiven. Waste not another day on sorrow, not another moment. Live happily, and be at peace."

Jack felt a strange something inside as he listened to Nick's quiet voice. It felt like shackles were corroding and falling away, and their leaden weight was releasing his heart and soul, and he was rising swiftly out of a cold and sunless place, and as he rose he could begin to see the light above him through the murky waters. Jack listened to the whispers like a child, with wide wondering eyes and open mouth. He laughed out loud when Nick told him who really killed the giant. And he cried tears of sympathy, of relief, of happiness, of peace. By the time Nick gave him Gullinda's message, he felt like he had broken through to the surface at last, out of the deep, and the sun was shining on him again, and for the first time in sixty years, he could breathe and laugh and *live*.

Jack gathered Nick up in a hug. Roland and Henry and Bill watched, enchanted, as the old man smiled a bright smile they had never seen before, a smile no living person had seen, and the old man and the boy laughed and danced and shouted with joy.

Jack suddenly stopped and gave Nick a serious look.

"But where's the treasure? Surely you've brought back some treasure!"

"I . . . I didn't steal any," said Nick.

"Ha! What kind of thief are you!" Jack beamed down at him. "Do you know what you really are, Nick?" he asked.

"No, sir," said Nick, a little bewildered.

Jack tousled his hair.

"You're a good lad."

● CHAPTER 21 ●

Roland took Finch's body out of the tree and dug a hole to bury him. They all gathered around the grave and Henry said a prayer.

Jack thought it would be unwise to leave the ogre's weapons lying about. His men loaded the cart with Gnasher's helmet and as many weapons as the horses could pull. The old man said they would return the next day to gather the rest.

There was food and drink in the wagon. Nick had not even considered how hungry he was during his frantic adventures on the cloud island. He wolfed down huge quantities of bread and cheese and salted meat, and guzzled mug after mug of cider.

Exhaustion overcame Nick as he ate. He fell asleep with a piece of bread in one hand and a mug in the other. Jack took these away and lay the boy down on a blanket, adding another on top to protect him from the coming chill of night.

Nick slept for a long time, dreaming about the cloud island. He sensed the wagon bouncing along the path, and woke up certain that he was back on the ogre's cart. Then he opened his eyes and saw stars overhead, flanked by the dark shapes of trees on either side of the forest road, and he remembered where he was. He felt the sweet relief that sleepers feel when they find that nightmares are only nightmares.

Nick wondered about Gullinda, and where she went after she escaped. Was she finding out now what lay beyond the mountain, what undiscovered mysteries? Then Nick slept again, deeper this time than the first, and far longer.

❦ CHAPTER 22 ❦

What to do, Gullinda wondered, about the great rope and the cart that held it to the cloud island. She spent the night pondering the question. As the stars swirled overhead, she paced around the massive vehicle, squinting through the darkness.

And what of Gnasher and Basher? Neither was there when she arrived. She had watched as the beanstalk toppled from the edge, its fingers tearing the boulder away as if to wield it as a weapon of destruction. Was that the end for one of her sons? For the sake of all the helpless, fragile folk who lived below, she hoped so.

Gnasher must have taken the rope down, she thought. She knew him well enough. Gnasher would send his brother down the beanstalk—because that was the dangerous way, the path that destroyed their father. And he would make a triumphant descent on his own invention. His arrogance wouldn't allow him to go any other way. When she put her hand on the heavy cord, she could almost feel Gnasher's evil presence far below. For a moment she even thought she heard his voice.

If all had gone well, if she had arrested his descent in time, Gnasher was trapped between worlds at the end of this rope. Too high to reach the world below. And too far down to climb back up—too far for Gnasher at least, who was powerful of mind but weak of body. It was a cruel end, but nothing compared to the punishment he was prepared to inflict on the little innocents.

What to do about the rope? She thought about prying up the spikes at the end of the chains and sending the whole accursed creation—rope, spool, and cart—over the side. But those spikes were driven deep into the rock, and she doubted if she could free them. Besides, it seemed a reckless gesture. What if Nick or some unlucky stranger was standing below?

Perhaps the best plan was to wait for several days, after Gnasher's strength gave out for sure, and he had fallen, and then remove the stone she had jammed into the gears and wind the rope up again.

The sun was rising. Its first modest light illuminated the horizon in the direction of the castle, but then the world spun lazily and the glow passed in front of her at the very spot where the rope disappeared over the edge.

The edge. She had been close to it before, but never dared to go all the way to the very brink, not even on that day when she hacked the beanstalk away so many years before. As always, the mist made it impossible to tell where solid ground ended. But now the end of the rope, where it bent and disappeared, clearly marked the spot where land stopped and the void began. Perhaps if she went there and stuck her head out, she could see the fabled land of little people, far below. Just one time, she would like to see it, the home of Jack and Nick.

She stood and walked cautiously through the mist, following the rope, testing each step before putting her weight down. When she was three steps away, she leaned out to look, but the fog still obscured her view.

Afraid now to be so close to the end of her world, she turned and walked sideways, extending one foot gingerly across the ground and then sliding the other behind.

She leaned as far as she dared. Out here, the wind was louder, whistling and moaning as it cut across the rocky shore. She looked into the mist that enshrouded the edge. Something *was* down there—not a faraway land, but a dark shape just below. A shape that moved.

A bloody hand came out of the mist and seized her ankle. Gullinda fell backward and landed hard on the jagged stones, sending mist billowing in every direction. She heard the word *"Motherrrr,"* a barely audible croak. The hand tugged on her ankle, and she slid toward the edge. She would have been pulled farther, but the grip was weak.

Gnasher's face rose out of the mist. He was panting and his tongue hung out between his sharp teeth. His hair was matted with perspiration. He looked up at

Gullinda and tried to smile. The expression seemed contrite at first, pleading and helpless. Then she looked past the smile and saw the truth that Gnasher could not mask.

She drew her free foot back and held it poised above his face. "No, Gallinor. Never again. You can't come back."

She did not have to strike him. The words were enough. Gnasher's strength was spent, and his grip failed. His hand slid down her ankle and over her foot, and his face sank abruptly into the mist. There was no sound for a moment, and then a scream, far, far, far below.

CHAPTER 23

Nick opened his eyes to the morning light. He was in a soft bed with plump pillows all around, in a handsome room that looked somehow familiar. The sun was just beginning to shine through the window, breaking up rain clouds that gathered during the night.

Nick leaned out the window and saw the white stone of Jack's fortress. Below him, Bill was pulling the ivy down from the wall. When he saw Nick, he held up a piece of the vine in his fist and shook it. Then he laughed. Nick grinned back and waved.

On a table next to the bed some fine new clothes were laid out for him. There was also a basin filled with water. Nick took off the black garments that the thieves had given him and left them in a pile. He splashed water on his face and tried to scrub off as much of the dirt as he could. When he was dressed, he opened the door and stepped out into the same hall he'd crept down two nights before. It all looked so different in the light.

✳ ✳ ✳

Nick found Jack downstairs in the kitchen. The old man was having breakfast with the little girl. The table was covered with fruits, toasted breads, cheese, meats, and something in a covered bowl that smelled wonderful.

"Join us, Nick!" Jack said cheerfully. "I think you and Ann have met before."

Nick remembered too well the look the girl gave him the last time he saw her, the one that shamed him when he was caught stealing in Jack's gallery. He knew she was watching him now, but he could barely muster the courage to return the glance. Slowly, shyly, he raised his eyes. And when he did, she graced him with a warm and welcome smile.

"Breakfast first," said Jack. "Let's fill that belly of yours, and then I want to hear the whole story. Beginning to end, everything you saw and did. Tell me about that band of ruffians you were mixed up with, about that pair of monsters we saw, and especially about the giantess."

"That will take a while, sir," said Nick.

"It can take as long as you want, Nick. I had just about run out of things to paint."

● CHAPTER 24 ●

The night after the beanstalk burned, clouds gathered overhead and a healing rain fell in the parched valley where the awesome plant had grown. The earth eagerly soaked up the moisture, as fast as the skies could deliver it, and the ground stopped smoldering at last.

A tiny vine poked through the charred soil and wriggled into the moonlight. At its tip, a pure white flower blossomed with miraculous speed. Then a pod emerged from the flower. It hung like a beacon, fat with beans, glowing with a milky green light in the cool black night.